*"AN ABSORBING NOVEL
WRITTEN WITH GREAT SKILL!"*
—Edmund Fuller
*Chicago Sunday Tribune*

The critic who wrote those lines in 1953, when
VOICES IN THE HOUSE was first published,
thought he was praising a novel by an author named
John Sedges. What he did not know then, but what
we do know today, is that John Sedges was a closely
guarded pseudonym for Pearl S. Buck, the only
American woman ever to win both the Pulitzer
Prize and the Nobel Prize for Literature.

Pearl Buck adopted the name John Sedges so that
she could write about the American scene with complete freedom. Known throughout the world for her
novels about China—*The Good Earth, Peony,
Pavilion of Women,* and others—she did not wish
her American novels to rest upon their immense
fame. To her delight, the John Sedges' books were
widely hailed and read without any critic or reader
knowing the true identity of their author.

VOICES IN THE HOUSE
was originally published by The John Day Company, Inc.

# Pearl S. BUCK

## Voices in the House

PUBLISHED BY POCKET BOOKS NEW YORK

VOICES IN THE HOUSE

John Day edition published March 1953

A *Pocket Book* edition

1st printing...........June, 1960
4th printing......September, 1969

This *Pocket Book* edition includes every word
contained in the original, higher-priced edition. It is printed
from brand-new plates made from completely reset, clear, easy-to-read
type. *Pocket Book* editions are published by Pocket Books, a division
of Simon & Schuster, Inc., 630 Fifth Avenue, New York, N.Y. 10020.
Trademarks registered in the United States and other countries.

L

Standard Book Number: 671-75398-3.
This *Pocket Book* edition is published by arrangement with The John
Day Company, Inc.
*Printed in the U.S.A.*

# Foreword

Some years ago I woke one morning to find myself strangely oppressed. I felt suddenly that I was no longer a free individual. I had been cast in a mold. I had written so many books about Chinese people that I had become known as a writer only about China. This was natural enough and nobody's fault. When I began to write I knew no people intimately except the Chinese. My entire life had been spent in China and beyond that in Asia. In midstream, however, I had transferred myself to the West and to my own country, the United States. Soon, since any writer writes out of his everyday environment, I began, however tentatively, to write about American people. I became thereby someone else.

This someone else, who now was also I, for the old self, the Asian self, continued to exist and will always continue, was, I repeat, oppressed. The oppression was the result of a determination on the part of my readers, sometimes loving, sometimes critical, to insist that there must be no other me than the one they had always known; that is to say, the Asian me. But here was the new American me, eager to explore and adventure among my own people. To provide freedom for this American me, pseudonymity was the answer. The writer must have a new name. I chose the name of John Sedges, a simple one, and masculine because men have fewer handicaps in our society than women have, in writing as well as in other professions.

My first John Sedges novel was *The Townsman*. It is a long book, a story of the West, Kansas in scene, to which state I had made many quiet visits. I was pleased when Kansans praised its authenticity. Its hero is a modest fellow who refuses to ride wild horses, be a cowboy, shoot pistols into the air, kill his enemies, find gold in any hills, destroy Indians, or even get drunk. He is content merely to become the solid founder of a city. The novel was well received by critics and sold to some tens of thousands of readers. It thus proved itself as a successful first novel by an unknown writer.

Four other novels were published under the name John Sedges, and guesses became rampant as to the author. No secrets in this world are kept forever. Somebody always knows and tells. And my two selves were beginning to merge. I was by now at home in my own country, my roots were digging deep, and I was becoming increasingly familiar with my own people. The protection of John Sedges was neither so necessary nor so effective as it had been. In Europe the John Sedges novels were openly sold as Pearl Buck books. I was moving toward freedom. The shield was no longer useful.

So John Sedges has served his purpose and may now be discarded and laid away in the silver foil of memory. I declare my independence and my determination to write as I please in a free country, choosing my material as I find it. People are people whether in Asia or America, as everybody knows or ought to know, and for me the scene is merely the background for human antics. Readers will still be the critics, of course, but I shall hope and strive to please and to amuse. Why else should books be written?

PEARL S. BUCK

# VOICES
# IN
# THE
# HOUSE

THE big house stood on the top of a flattened hill outside the town of Manchester, Vermont. It was an ancient house, built nearly one hundred years before the last Mrs. Winsten died and before William Asher married her daughter Elinor and changed it to the Asher house. It was not entirely changed at that, old Vermonters still called it the Winsten House and always would. William did not resent this for he liked the house as it always had been. He was not afraid of losing his identity, it did not occur to him that such a thing could happen. He was large enough in mind to be himself under all circumstances, and so to enjoy Elinor's heritage and make it his own. There was an Asher house on Long Island which he could have had, as an only child, had he wanted it. But he had learned in his childhood, in the soft green summers in Vermont, to love the town of Manchester and the graceful mountains about it, and he sold the Long Island house without compunction when his parents died.

The Winsten house itself had been built so large and solid that the following generations of the family had not added so much as a wing to it. Before its founder, Adam Winsten, had died, in the early years of the nineteenth century, he had needed a big house, for he begat a family of twelve children, nine of whom lived to grow up. Most of the grandchildren, however, had gone West. The house, huge as it was, could not contain them, and in the West, grown rich on gold and railroads, they had all but forgotten that they had come from Vermont. Yet in the earlier century there was always one Winsten to live on in the house, and old Mr. Winsten, the last of them and Elinor's father, as lean and wintry before he died as an aging elm tree, had been an Adam, too. But none of his sons wanted a house so big that new servants would not stay after one look at the stretching roofs, and none, neither son nor wife, wanted old Bertha, the cook who had lived in the house for as long as any of them could remember.

In the end the children all went away except Elinor, the youngest, and she stayed on with her mother and old Cousin Emma, who had always lived in the big house. It was during these years in the summers that William fell in love. He and Elinor were married soon and very quietly after Mrs. Asher died of a stroke one spring day, when she had worked too long over her rose beds. Cousin Emma announced after the wedding that she had always wanted to live in New York, and now she would do so, since Jessica, who was the dead Mrs. Winsten, had willed her enough money.

This left the house to Elinor and therefore to William who liked the idea of living in it. The Ashers had always been merely a summer family, so far as Vermont was concerned, and William loved Vermont and hated being a transient. New-fledged from Harvard Law School, he had opened his first small office in Manchester and there it still was, for sentiment's sake, for now, years later, as a successful lawyer, he was compelled to have his main office in New York. Between New York and Boston it had been difficult to choose, but the Ashers were a New York family and to continue his business life there made a nice balance beween the past and the present.

2

The big house remained exactly as it had always been. On the outside it was white clapboard and green shutters, but underneath the wood the walls were of brick, and so the windows had deep sills. The house stretched long and not quite symmetrical, two wings on one side and three on the other, all set back some feet from the central part, which was three stories high and severely plain except for the carved front door. A long driveway of elm trees, now so old that William had them regularly inspected and reinforced every autumn before the winter winds came down from the mountains, led to the lawn before the house. The first Adam had planted the elms widely apart so that the driveway was spacious and lent its space to the house. When the front door opened it revealed the same instinct for space within. A wide hall ran straight through the house to a glass door at the back, which opened upon an enclosed garden. Double stairways joined above the door, and to the right and left were what had always been called, since the first Adam's day, the east and west parlors.

The furnishings were still fine, the pleasant mixture of an old family who bought the things they liked in each generation and put them together without thought of periods. Elinor had considered the rooms overfurnished when she became the mistress, and she had invited her brothers and sisters, scattered over distant states, to take certain pieces for their own homes as mementos of their common childhood. The mahogany velvet-covered chairs and sofas and the special pieces which had always been in the house, such as the long French mirrors between the front windows in the parlors, of course no one thought of taking away, any more than they would have thought of digging up by the roots the old syringas and lilacs, or the vast elms themselves. Certain things belonged in the big house and the Winstens had proper respect for them.

3

## Voices in the House

The house had not seemed strange to William Asher when he moved into it as a bridegroom, that late spring day, now twenty-five years ago. He had been in and out of the house every summer of his youth. Elinor's brothers had been his friends and in that sense he had grown up with her, only gradually aware, as summers passed, that he was falling in love with her. Thus, too, he had grown used to Bertha, and her husband, Heinrich, who was the butler, and it was not strange to have them as his servants after his marriage. It had not been so easy to get used to their daughter Jessica, however, born to Bertha and Heinrich the year after William and Elinor were married. For the two stout elderly servants to have an unexpected child was preposterous, they felt it so and were embarrassed and confounded. Elinor had laughed a great deal, but she gave them permission when they asked to name the child Jessica, after the dead Mrs. Winsten, her mother. And so the strange little Jessica had grown up in the kitchen, on the fringe of the big house, although William was scarcely aware of her existence, except to wonder sometimes, when he caught a glimpse of her, what would become of her. She was a servant's child and yet it was difficult to think of her as such. She was quite exquisite as she grew out of babyhood, very slender, her eyes electric blue, her fine-spun hair as yellow as the traditional gold.

Once years ago, when he came home, William had walked through the unlocked door to find Jessica in the east parlor, a child then of seven, but with a duster in her hand, for Bertha was already teaching her to help. She was not using the duster, however. She was sitting on one of the rose velvet chairs, her eyes unseeing and bright, her lips upcurved in a vague sweet smile, as she gesticulated with the hand that held no duster, a delicate

4

child's hand, white and soft and not at all a housemaid's hand.

When William stared she recovered herself with a gasp.

"Oh, Mr. Asher, I never heard you," she whispered. She jumped from the chair and ran to the kitchen, while he called to her not to mind. She was only a child, and although he had been afraid of children until his own were born, he did not like to frighten so tender and pretty a little creature. But she did not return. The next week Bertha sent her away to a convent in Canada, an English convent, where the nuns, she told Elinor, would be more strict than French nuns.

"Jessica is so little to be sent away," Elinor had said half remorsefully when she told William.

"Too young," he agreed.

Nothing could change Bertha's mind, however, and they let Jessica go. They were young themselves in those days, they were deeply engrossed in their own life and love. Jessica came home sometimes in the summers, yet never to stay long. Bertha found her troublesome and when Heinrich died in the year that Jessica was ten, Bertha let her spend even the vacations in the convent, until she was old enough to leave for good and work as a maid in the big house. As a maid, they were all used to her now, although, as Elinor said, Jessica would never be as steady as Bertha and probably she needed to get married. Still, as Elinor had said again only this morning, who was there to marry Jessica except Herbert, the chauffeur and houseman, who had come seven years or so ago, after a succession of unsatisfactory substitutes for Heinrich? He had fallen in love with Jessica at once in his slow stubborn way, and for love he had stayed on in the big house, in spite of her persistent, half-laughing, half-angry refusals.

This servant gossip, as William called it, was merely

mild diversion and subject for Elinor's sprightly and humorous description when he came home tired from the office. He listened, only partly heeding, as a form of relaxation, while she put the children to bed. Now of course the children were grown up, Winsten married and Edwin and Susan away at college. He and Elinor were alone again in the big house.

The train, swinging between the Vermont hills, stopped with a jerk at the station, and William gathered his papers together, slipped them into his black leather briefcase, and prepared to get out at once. Elinor had given him the briefcase last Christmas, and it had then been brown. The difference between brown and black, in a lawyer's briefcase, is delicate but profound, and William, gazing at the new briefcase, had betrayed his own doubt.

Elinor had laughed. "Give it back to me," she cried, her blue eyes sparkling in frosty mirth. "Give it back to me, William, and I'll exchange it for a black one. You've had black ever since I knew you and I wondered what effect change would have upon you."

"It is not a question of the effect on me," he had replied. "I am concerned with the effect on others. Clients expect a certain sobriety."

To this Elinor had returned nothing but her smile, sweet beneath the sparkling eyes. He was relieved, however, when a few days later he had found the handsome black briefcase, his initials impressed upon it in pale gold.

Herbert had asked for the day off, which explained the coming home by train. It was pleasant to look out of the car window, however, and see Elinor, waiting for him on the platform. She was here to meet him, driving the car herself, and she was still, after twenty-five years of marriage, a pleasant sight to him. She had come in her own car, a small dark green convertible, which however she never converted. Today at the end of summer the windows were rolled down, but the top remained fixed. She sat in the front seat, smoking a cigarette in the offhand dainty sort of way which was natural to her, a slender, rather tall woman, who had never cut her blonde hair. It was soft, almost straight, and now, although she was only forty-five, it was growing white, and because it had been so blonde, he scarcely noticed it, knotted heavily at her neck as she had always worn it. Had she not been so dainty, so thin, so fine-boned, she might, he sometimes felt, have looked a slattern. As it was, the slight disorder always apparent about her person seemed accidental. He had learned not to point out that the top button of her white silk blouse was open, revealing the glimpse of a bosom surprisingly young. He knew that to remind her was to risk a smile, a shrug, certainly not the button buttoned. A pin, one of the many brooches he had given to her, would have taken the place of the stitch or two needed to tighten the buttonhole. She would probably never take the stitch, he now knew.

"Herbert not back yet?" he inquired as he got into the car, his eyes averted. She slid over, yielding the wheel to him. It was accepted between them that he was the better driver because he was more steady and because the late afternoon traffic did not annoy him. Manchester in summer was a tourists' town, highly refined, of course, but tourist in spite of that. The Equinox Hotel was filled with the best people, but Cook's tours in buses screeched in the streets while others found less expensive hostels.

"I came alone because I wanted to tell you—Jessica has decided to marry Herbert," Elinor said.

"No!"

"Yes, she has at last. They were away all day together."

He swung down the street to the right, and after some

blocks turned into a road which, after two miles of silence and green, gave into their own lane.

"After seven years," he murmured, amazed.

"I always knew that Herbert would get her in the end," Elinor said.

"I wonder if she really wants to marry Herbert," William mused, not caring. It was a delight always renewed to drive toward the massive house on the hill ahead, and he slowed the car.

"Don't talk about Herbert as a husband," Elinor said, rather sharply.

William smiled. Elinor was too fastidious, she did not like Herbert, and the less because she could really find no fault with him. He was an exemplary character, faithful, honest, silent, hardworking, and burning with secret energy. It had not taken her long to discover that this energy was directed to a relentless pursuit of Jessica.

William remembered. "Six years ago this summer, I believe it was, you told me that Herbert was in love with Jessica and that she hated him."

Elinor reminded him. "You said that it was a pity he wasted his efforts, and I told you that if he kept on he would win."

He turned his head to glance at her profile and saw it enigmatic, her delicate lips severe, her eyes doubtful, her eyebrows lifted. The wind was blowing back soft strands of her hair leaving her forehead bare. She had a high forehead, not knobby, but intelligent and beautiful. The look meant that she preferred not to talk about the matter any more. He fell silent, knowing that when she was inclined she would talk, explaining herself fully without being urged.

He swept the car gently into the driveway, stopped it at precisely the proper spot, opened the door for Elinor, and got out on the other side. At this moment Herbert

8

came from the house by the pantry entrance and took over the car. He was still in his best double-breasted blue suit.

"Good evening, Mr. Asher," he said.

"Good evening, Herbert," William replied. He paused, his foot on the lowest step to the columned porch. The columns had been added to the house only fifty years ago by Elinor's grandfather. "I hear you're to be congratulated," he went on.

Herbert's face did not deepen its usual brickish red. "Jessica gave me her word today," he said. He had a lipless mouth but his small greyish eyes were not unkind.

"Well, well," William said. "You've been very faithful."

"I never looked at another woman," Herbert said. His voice, flat and firm, suited his square-set body. Dutch ancestors somewhere, William thought, had given him the blockhouse build, the thick hands.

William smiled and mounted the steps and Herbert drove the car away to the garage. Elinor was already in the house, she had run up the marble steps while they talked, as light and fleet as ever she had been. He saw no glimpse of her, however. She was already in the kitchen or upstairs or in the garden and he entered his silent house. He did not mind the absence of his children, knowing that they were at the unreachable age, lost in a time tunnel out of which they would emerge when they were fully adult, as Winsten was beginning to do. He could talk to his elder son as to a man, but Edwin was still impossibly young and opinionated. Susan as a woman he felt he did not know and the child she had been was gone altogether. He took Elinor's word for it that she was all that he hoped she was and meanwhile he enjoyed the fact that she was certainly very pretty, although he regretted that she had not inherited her mother's permanently slender figure. Susan looked like his side of the family. She was dark and inclined to be plump, and she would have to look after her diet, as he had learned to do. He had once let himself get fat in his thirties and it had taken Elinor's repulsion to alarm him enough to bring himself down. Not so long as he lived would he forget that midnight scene.

"You don't love me as you used to, Elinor." He had said that because she turned her head away.

"Oh well—" she had murmured.

Desire, rising toward high tide, had suddenly ebbed. He seized her chin.

"Look here, tell me the truth!"

She had been ashamed to tell him but she did it somehow, because he forced her, and that night for the first time he began to understand the difference between himself and Elinor, the dividing difference, indeed, between man and woman. Her passion was a secret silver spring permeating all her being, connecting nerves and feelings, while his was a river, separate and strong. The river flowed in him independent of all else, determined upon its own course, but anywhere the spring in her could be stopped by distaste, by moods, by thoughts she concealed.

The boys took after the Winstens, through some perversity of inheritance they were tall, fair and extremely handsome, unnecessarily so, especially Edwin. But Susan had dark curly hair. He was very fond of Susan, with a peculiar secret fondness which he excused on the grounds that she was his only daughter.

At the top landing he met Jessica. She appeared at her usual speed, a slight creature, flying down the long wide hall, her pale green uniform fluttering, her white apron ruffling and the bows at her back all ends and ribbons. She was only twenty-four and looked much younger.

"Don't hurry, Jessica," he warned her. "You'll fall down the stairs one of these days."

"Oh, I don't mind what happens to me, Mr. Asher," she

replied. Her hands were full of fresh towels, she was
putting away the laundry, and the smell of clean ironed
linen was about her like a fragrance. She was shining
clean, her blonde braids wrapped tight about her head
and little damp sweat curls encircled her face.

"Always in a hurry," he grumbled. "You make me tired
just to look at you. So you are to marry Herbert, after
all these years!"

She laughed suddenly. "Oh, that man! I have to get
rid of him somehow. It's Mother's doing, really. She says
it's time. I might as well marry him as anybody."

She was a creature so childlike, though woman grown,
that instinctively one felt playful merely at the sight of
her. Her uniforms, pale blue or pink or green, her little
ruffled white aprons and caps, made her as unreal as a
servant on a stage.

"I don't know that you can get rid of a man by
marrying him," he said rather more seriously than he
felt.

"Oh, at least he won't keep asking me," she retorted.
She spoke English with a clear pure accent, the result
of her years in the convent. Bertha still had a guttural
German edge to her tongue and Heinrich had never mas-
tered the English language at all. But this child of theirs
spoke with a silvery sweet voice and a carved beauty of
words. He had once said to Elinor that Jessica had come
from the convent speaking English like an angel and she
had said, "Do angels speak English?"

"Tongues," he had replied, "of which English is doubtless the most beautiful." He liked good English, he was
somewhat precious about literature, and often felt that
had he taken the time he might have been a writer.

"Well, I suppose you know what you are doing," he
now grumbled to Jessica who stood with her arms full

11

of the fragrant linen. "All young people seem to think they do, anyhow."

He went on to his room where everything was laid out as usual for his bath and change. Jessica did that for him and for Elinor and they would miss her, unless, of course, she kept on working, which he supposed she would not. Herbert Morris would not want his wife working even though he would probably ask for a raise on the strength of getting married.

He averted his mind from the thought of Herbert Morris married to Jessica. There was something distasteful about the involuntary picture which crept into his mind like the unrolling of a secret film, that solid brutish body fastened upon the pale delicacy of Jessica. He was shocked at his own imagination. Civilized as he believed himself to be, the antics of the human brain were distressing. He had no wish, indeed, to imagine Herbert Morris in any way whatever, and he felt only the utmost repulsion toward the fellow except as he daily appeared, respectable and decent in his chauffeur's uniform, or houseman's coat. So far as he was concerned, this was the only Herbert Morris there was. Nor, for that matter, did he have the slightest interest in the pale delicacies of the maid Jessica. He was, he believed, a man of clean heart and this by choice and taste, yet here was his antic mind, and if his mind could so exhibit its inner lawlessness, the inward brute, he supposed and most unwillingly acknowledged, what must other minds be, less controlled than his?

It did not bear consideration. He dismissed the matter by turning his thoughts firmly to the clear and bodiless aspects of the law. He was at this time involved in an interesting case which concerned the claims of two inventors, who unfortunately had produced almost identical improvements in machinery for the treatment of drying woolens. Independent of each other and unknown, the two minds had followed strangely similar paths. Which had begun first the thought process and how inexorable was it that one had been shrewd enough to reach the goal of the patent office first? In such cool rumination, he finished the changing of his garments and went down to dinner with a mood both pleasant and calm. Jessica and Herbert were only servants again.

Immediately he received a shock. As he came downstairs, his step noiseless upon the carpet, he saw Jessica. Taking advantage, he supposed, of the space of time before dinner while she waited for them to appear, she was in the east parlor, sitting in the rose velvet chair. It was not only this. She had taken off her apron and her cap and she had moved the chair so that she could see herself in the long French mirror between the windows. She had even changed her hair somehow, it stood about her face in a fluffy yellow cloud, and she was talking in a low musical conversational voice almost distinctly. He paused on the stair, remembering with some indignation, the same scene years ago, which, he supposed, had made Bertha decide on the convent. But this was worse. Jessica was actually speaking words of love to some unseen person.

"But, my darling," she was saying, "don't you see that I love you? Everything I do is for you. This house, the gardens, myself, would I care for it all as I do if it were not for you? Would I stay here when I could be in England or France or Italy, if it were not for you?"

She laughed softly for someone, shook back her hair and reached out her arms.

This was monstrous, he thought in consternation. He was very glad that Elinor had not seen it. He came forward firmly, and Jessica hearing his step turned with a flying movement of terror.

13

"Oh, it's you—" she breathed.

Her face went absolutely white, a bluish white, she snatched at her cap and apron and put them on with swift and trembling hands.

"Were you imagining yourself in a play?" he inquired not unkindly.

She looked at him as though she did not comprehend. "Please, please don't tell anybody!" she whispered.

"Then you think you were doing wrong?" he asked.

"Please!" she begged.

"You are very foolish," William said severely.

Again she threw him that fearful uncomprehending look and fled away, kitchenward. He stood frowning for a moment, pursing his firm mouth, then he decided to let the moment pass. What Jessica was saying before the mirror was too silly to repeat even to Elinor.

In the kitchen Herbert and Bertha looked at Jessica as she dashed in, her cap awry, her apron crooked.

"You look like somebody was chasin' you," Herbert said in a fond effort to amuse her.

"I ran downstairs too fast," she said, trying to control her quick breathing.

"Always she runs," Bertha complained. "What for? It don't make some sense."

But the atmosphere was benign. They were not going to scold, Jessica could see, not today, and turning her back on them she began to place the bouillon cups on the silver tray.

Her life was distinct and separate from the rest of the house, a life within a life, and the two worlds meeting only at the points of service had nothing to do with each other spiritually. Bertha, large, sensible, firm-faced in her grey cotton uniform, sat at the kitchen table, slicing roast beef for Herbert. Jessica still did not sit down.

On every table in the kitchen the dishes were in disorder, but the oblong center table was set with straw mats and the red-handled kitchen knives and forks. Herbert sat at the end which had been Heinrich's place when he was alive. Upon the day, now six years ago when Bertha told Herbert to sit there, he knew that she was on his side. Six long years it had taken to persuade Jessica that he was going to marry her, seven years he had been after her, but now that he looked back, he felt that if Heinrich had not died, he would still have been in pursuit and she would still not have given in. Her father was always on Jessica's side, no matter what she wanted.

"Sit down, girl," he ordered her.

Jessica sat down and began to eat daintily from the plate her mother had piled too high. Never could her mother learn that the sight of too much food sickened her and long ago she had ceased complaining.

"Miss Elinor told me I should fetch up a bottle of champagne to wish luck," Bertha said now.

She got up, heavy on her feet, and waddled to the refrigerator where the bottle was cooling.

"Ah," Herbert said wiping his mouth with the back of his hand. "That was nice of her. Next to beer, I don't know but what champagne is as good as you can get. A cold glass of beer is always my favrit, but that's not saying I'm against the champagne for once."

"Jessica, liebchen, eat," Bertha commanded. "It iss a big day for die alte mutter."

Jessica looked up, uncertain, quivering, slight, conscious of the two faces turned toward her, each with its peculiar and terrifying yearning, as though, she thought, she were a mouse and they were large affectionate cats. She smiled a quick and brilliant smile, her armor of defense.

"Oh, I'm eating, Mother," she cried in her sweet voice,

15

and she continued to smile while her mother poured the sparkling wine into the second best goblets.

They held their glasses high in the German fashion, Herbert self-conscious, embarrassed, unable to share in Bertha's open sentimental mood.

"Here's to you, my children," Bertha said. "Be happy, dear ones, and give me grandchildren. Herbert, be good to my liebchen, and Jessica, you be a good wife like I teached you."

They drank, Bertha solemnly and slowly, Herbert in gulps, and Jessica in quick sips.

"Ah," Bertha said, setting down her empty glass. "I think of der lieber fater. How happy today would he be, Jessica!"

"Don't talk about him," Jessica said sharply.

"No, no," Bertha agreed. "Nothing sad today. It is right. Eat now, liebchen."

She took her own knife and fork again and cut the roast beef upon her plate into large square bits and began solidly to eat her dinner.

Herbert did not talk while he ate. He had grown up on a farm where conversation was not to be thought of with food. He clutched his fork upright in his left hand while he sawed the beef with his knife, held in his right. Jessica looked away. When they were married she would tell him that the fork was not held so. But then he had not had the opportunity to learn such things that she had. She waited at the table and saw how people held their forks, people who knew.

Mr. Asher used his fork and knife so nicely, eating in a way that was never repulsive. She had always liked Mr. Asher, even when she was only a child. His marriage to Miss Elinor was a real romance, like in fairy books, the handsome dark young man, well mannered, his voice pleasant, and nothing repulsive about him. She looked at her plate steadily now while she ate, taking the smallest bites, careful not to look at Herbert or her mother, who were repulsive when they ate. But she was twenty-four already, and no one else had asked her to marry him, because she had never let anyone ask, for who had there been except butcher boys and grocery clerks and shop-keepers? Herbert, too, she had tried to prevent from the very first, six years ago, but he was not to be prevented. He was always about and he simply kept saying the same thing over and over again, and her mother telling her that she must marry somebody and so why not Herbert because he was solid and good. They could live on the chicken farm and Herbert would look after things in the evenings. It would make a home for all of them, even for her mother when she got too old to work any more.

"Dondt pick, Jessie," her mother said sharply at this moment. "You eat good now, like I tell you."

Immediately all appetite left her. When she was small, a pale little girl, always too thin, her mother had pushed food into her mouth and held it there, her big flat palm tight over her mouth to keep her from spitting it out. Once she had bitten her mother's palm and her mother had slapped her mouth until it bled, and then her front teeth were loose for a while. Yet she knew her mother loved her. Her mother loved her terribly, terribly, and that was why it was so wicked not to love her back.

Herbert held a fork full of food, poised, "You want to put some meat on your bones. You'd feel a lot better."

"Oh, I feel well enough," she said, laughing.

The bell rang from the dining room and she darted up and flew to the door. "Ah, they're ready," she cried.

"She'll settle down once she's married," Bertha said.

"She'll have to," Herbert said.

"Her father was flightylike," Bertha went on, "he was immer so qvick changing, and fussy, too. I settled him,

17

when we was married, ya, yust like I settle Jessie too,
when she comes here. She lissens to me, and she lissens
to you, you vill see."

"All the same," Herbert said, "I'll be good to her."

"Sure," Bertha said, "I am good also. Vy not? She iss
all I have."

Autumn was the season that William liked best of all
the year. He had never been an enthusiast for spring,
although it had been spring when he fell in love with
Elinor. Because it was spring he had distrusted the violent
attraction he felt the moment he saw her that summer
when he was twenty-two, especially as he had seen her
every summer for years before without thinking of love.
He had even been mildly in love with someone quite
different the summer before. Marian Heyworth was a
neighbor, a nice girl, he still thought, when occasionally
he remembered her, not with any interest but with placid
wonder at the turn his life had taken. The Heyworths
had owned a summer place next to theirs in Manchester
and Marian was decent about Elinor after the first shock.
Indeed, it had been her accusation that had revealed to
William the full enormity of his new passion. He was of
a dogged nature, however, and when she faced him with
the truth he acknowledged it.

"I think you're right, Marian," he had said. "I regret it
very much but it has happened."

He had never regretted it, of course. Elinor was not
only his wife, she was still his beloved, a very rare combination, he believed, after so many years. But he had
not allowed himself to speak his love until after the summer was well begun. In the dogdays, hot and humid, on
a particularly uncomfortable day when they had paddled
down the upper reaches of the brook near the house, he
had proposed and been accepted promptly. Elinor had

18

not seemed surprised. When he inquired why not, she had said in a matter-of-fact voice, "I've been expecting it, William. Marian told me that you had told her."

He had been shocked at this frankness between the two girls he knew best but he said nothing. Men would never have spoken of such sacred matters but he knew now that to women nothing was sacred. He winced when he thought of it, but he knew it was true. Elinor's bridge parties confirmed his conviction. Quite against his will he had sometimes overheard the remarks of the seven women in and about Manchester who were her best friends, whose seven husbands were also his best friends in the country club, and he was always shocked. He did not believe that Elinor was so wickedly frank as the seven unwise wives, but he did not dare to ask. He simply went on believing that she was not, because he considered her unique among women and very near perfection. Her graceful head, poised upon a rather long slender neck, the soft silver-gold knot of hair at the nape, to this day sent a ripple of delight through his blood. He could not keep from touching her when he passed her, his hand smoothing the hair to the contour of her head, or pressing the firmness of her small breasts.

Autumn, then, was his favorite season, the early autumn, beginning, here in Vermont, somewhere in late August and ending with the first snowfall. In his way he was an outdoor man, not hunting or shooting, but enjoying the shallow curves of the pleasant mountains, the change of color upon the trees. This morning when he came downstairs he saw a tiny grey feather lying on the rust brown carpet of the living room and he stooped and picked it up. It was the feather of some small wild bird, the wind had blown it in when the door was opened, perhaps by Jessica when she was sweeping. But how delightful to live in a big house where yet one could find upon the carpet the feather of a bird! He put the feather between the leaves of the book lying on his special reading table, the current book which he now read as he waited for Elinor to come down to breakfast. It happened to be Proust, and it pained him to realize how remote the story was, how far from France today, or from life in any part of the world, indeed. He felt the permanent hidden nostalgia that all men of his age feel, he supposed, for the era they knew as young men, the safe, assured, happy years which unaccountably had simply ceased to be. In his way he had been a young radical, alarming his parents as today he was alarmed by Winsten and Edwin, not because they were radical, far from it, but because they were so conservative, so prudent, so dangerously careful not to ally themselves with the slightest possibility of revolt. Two safer young men than his sons never lived, and he hid from them his own doubts and queries, as a liberal. He still classified himself as a liberal, a conservative liberal, of course, but certainly a liberal, a point of view which disgusted his sons. Susan so far had shown no interest in politics or the world, or in anything except herself and her chances of marriage. It mortified him sometimes to see how single-mindedly she pursued her quest of a mate. Surely Elinor had not been so obvious or so determined. Above all, Susan detested, despised was her word, the women who in the past had devoted their lives to feminism, or as he preferred to put it, to the equality of the sexes. His own grandmother had been a friend and helper of Elizabeth Cady Stanton but Susan begged him not to remind her of it. Among the family photographs was a picture of the two ladies taken together, in hooped skirts and side curls, and Susan, coming once upon the likeness of her ancestress, had expressed fierce scorn.

"Women like that have set us back so far with men that we can't mend the damage!"

"Explain yourself," he had demanded.

"Don't you see, Dad?" Susan had cried. "They made men hate us!"

"Rubbish," he had retorted. "I don't hate any woman."

"You wouldn't like me to be a lawyer, would you?" she asked too shrewdly.

"I don't think you'd make a good one," he countered. "You haven't a logical mind."

"There," she said in triumph, "I told you! If it hadn't been for the Stanton woman and her kind you wouldn't have thought about my mind and I'd have been what I liked."

"Do you wish to be a lawyer?" he had asked after a digesting pause.

"No, of course not," she had said with outrageous calm. "That was just a catch."

He gave up. He could make nothing of this generation. Serious conversation was impossible with them. They sacrificed their very souls for a wisecrack, a form of speech which he loathed as destructive not only of sensible communication but of civilization itself.

Elinor came down at this moment and he put down the book and showed her the minute grey feather.

"See what I found upon the floor, blown hither by the autumn wind."

She looked at it and smiled absently. "It's only a sparrow feather, I'm afraid. Probably two sparrows had a fight—they're always quarreling in the gutters under the roof."

He put it back between the leaves without reply. There were times when she caught his moods perfectly, replying so delicately true that he could not refrain from taking her in his arms. At other times, as now, she refused com-

21

pliance. He understood exactly what she meant. Her mood this morning was remote, she was to be let alone, he must not kiss her close, she was off somewhere in the day to come, living ahead without him, and he might or might not know about it. It had taken him a long time, at least ten years, to comprehend that marriage consisted largely of mutual consideration of the other's mood, selfishly perhaps, in order to keep within the circle together. They had clashed a good deal in the early years, because he had taken it for granted that a wife was supposed—not, of course, to obey her husband, but at least to consider him before she considered herself. He knew now that Elinor with all her delicacy was of tougher fiber than he, that she could do without him better than he without her, and that she could be most cruelly stubborn about letting him suffer it out.

He suspected that what was true of Elinor was true of all women. They could and did manage their own lives, either openly and above board as Elinor did or else secretly. Yet he was completely happy with her, sometimes to his own surprise, and he was still infatuated with her, although there were times when she made him thoroughly angry.

They sat down at the breakfast table, a rite which he always enjoyed so much that he felt sorry for his friends whose wives did not rise from bed in time to share this hour. Elinor enjoyed it, too, and did this morning, for in spite of the remoteness of her mood she got up to kiss the top of his head when it became apparent that he was not going to kiss her. He had learned to leave her alone when she was remote, and here was his reward, that she would, as now, come fluttering back, even if only for something so light, so scarcely felt, so almost worthless, and yet so valued, as a kiss on top of his hair. He restrained himself from seizing her while she was near,

22

and was again rewarded by her kindling gaze when she sat down.

"I do like that grey suit with that maroon tie," she exclaimed.

"Thank you," he said calmly. "I rather like it myself."

Breakfast then went its usual way. They had faced each other, had taken temperatures, had renewed their mutual approval and understanding. He left the house for his Manchester office a few minutes later, and in spite of her somewhat warming good-by kiss, he was able to put his entire mind on his work. His marriage was entirely successful and therefore safe.

The house which he had left in such peace in the morning was in a roil when he returned to it in the evening. Elinor met him at the door with her finger on her lip and a warning glance toward the kitchen.

"What is the matter now?" he inquired in something less than his ordinary voice.

"Bertha is angry at Jessica again," Elinor sighed. "Neither of them will talk about it. Jessica is upstairs with her door locked, and Bertha is glowering over the stove."

He was not as patient with servants as Elinor was, although he recognized that this patience, inherited from the Winstens, was rewarded by the clinging loyalty of Bertha. Forty years had imbedded Bertha deeply into the family, like a pearl in an oyster, as valuable generally and yet as irritating, he sometimes felt, as the pearl must undoubtedly be.

"Herbert didn't say anything," he said, considering. Herbert all the way home had been simply the block-backed figure in the chauffeur's seat.

"Perhaps he doesn't know," Elinor said.

"Come, come," he said, putting his arm about her. "You must not let servants upset you." He was glad he had not told her of the scene of Jessica before the mirror.

"I don't think so of Bertha and Jessica," she replied.

"Once you let servants become human beings," he retorted, "you are in for trouble. There are other cooks as good as Bertha."

"Poor Bertha," Elinor said, but she relaxed pleasantly in his arm as they walked toward the living room. There she had set out the tray for cocktails, a task which was Jessica's but which she had performed as a matter of course when Jessica locked herself up.

"Shake it well, my love," he said. She had taken the frosted cocktail shaker. "Meanwhile I shall tidy myself a bit. I am sorry I am late."

When he came down again, tidied, Herbert was waiting in his white coat, and the house to all outward appearance was as usual upon a fine autumn evening. The doors were open to the dining room, two places were set at the table. He had thought, when the children went away to school, that he and Elinor would be lonely, the house so large and, always before filled with children, now so silent, so seemingly empty. He had discovered after a very few days that his apprehensions were unnecessary. The house was delightfully quiet, he did not miss the loud young voices, the poundings of footsteps upon the stairs, the shouts from the upper windows. It was pleasurable to wander through the rooms, orderly at last, to find a book where he had put it down, and no litter of comic magazines. Only at night sometimes, when sleepless he prowled about the house, did he see the small ghosts of the living children, Winsten at ten, a blond slip of a boy, always leaping, running, darting through the halls; Edwin, the brown boy, deep in a chair in the library, a particular chair, his head bent over a book, his features foreshortened. Many a time when he himself had sat in the chair it was still warm from the body of his son. And the ghost of Susan, flesh of his flesh, yet female and alien to him eternally, they all came back in the night, the children they once had been, and he yearned over them and then he felt old age loom near because they were gone. For though they came home at Christmas and in the summer, it was no real homecoming. The house for them was now only a brief stopping place on the way to the final destination. They were not lost to him, for he had had them, newborn and helpless, the little children learning to walk and talk, and then impetuous school children, and turbulent in adolescence. Those were the children he kept and he did not miss the tall and gawky young adults who came back so briefly to use his house as a place to bathe and change before dances and dinners, a place where they slept and ate without paying for it. He had wondered sometimes as they grew what they thought of him and their mother, and whether they missed at all the early closeness. Watching them, he had decided that they missed nothing, and that they did not think. They were on their way to unknown places, blown by the winds of their own desires.

Still, this was only his night mood. In the morning he woke up, rested by silence, and when he was bathed and dressed his reflection in the mirror was not at all that of an aging man. Quite otherwise, he looked what he was, a man in the prime of his life, his hair scarcely grey except at the temples, and without a hint of baldness. But he inherited his thatchy hair, a brush until he had found a barber in the city who knew how to subdue it by skilful cutting. . . . No, he did not miss the children. Being alone with Elinor renewed his ardor.

"Are you thinking of the children?" Elinor inquired too shrewdly.

"How did you know?" he asked. He was accustomed to this second sight, this intuition, telepathy, whatever it was that she possessed, but he no longer feared it or resented it, as he had once done when they were young. He had yielded himself to his marriage years ago, and now there was nothing in him to hide, not even the will, once so stubborn, to maintain at least his own individuality.

"I know your father look." Her voice was tender with that special tenderness of which he had once been so jealous, because, it had seemed to him in the years of his youth when he could never possess enough of her, that she loved the children more than she did him.

"I was wondering if they miss us at all," he said.

"Of course not," she replied. "If they missed us it would simply mean that they were in retreat."

He went on to confess his guilt. "Then I suppose it is not wrong that I do not miss them. It seems pleasant to be alone with you in the house, as we were before they were born."

The house then had seemed to him far too large, and he had been eager to see it filled with children. Now it did not seem too large, perhaps because of the small and lively ghosts whom he could summon by a moment's memory. Life had been lived here and was therefore still alive. Yet he and Elinor were very different from the two young creatures who had come here newly married. They were facing life again, but what life? He had not been quite sure, when the children left, what adjustments aging lovers must make, and whether his reviving ardor would be acceptable to her. But he had faith in her. That was his comfort. He knew men who dreaded getting old with their wives. How fortunate was he that still above all other companions he found Elinor the best, not merely because he loved her but because her mind met his own. She was not a learned woman and she pretended no interest in the law, for which he was grateful, but her judgments were fresh, her approach to human beings was original and direct, and she never lied to him.

"Do you not miss the children?" he asked somewhat tentatively. He had avoided the question until now.

She gazed for a few seconds into the clear amber drink she held aloft, examining its color with pleasure. A sensuous creature, he thought, finding an absorbing delight in shape and color, and never ashamed of physical enjoyment, even of food. Her literalness, her natural lack of shame, perhaps, were what kept her younger than her years. Nothing dried the blood like false respectability, a tendency toward prudery against which he himself struggled because he dreaded the possibility of seeming ridiculous. He could never, for example, have belonged to one of those organizations which compelled its members to garb themselves in pseudo-Oriental robes and when, as had happened last week in New York, such an organization held its annual meeting in the city, so that he was compelled to see the antics of bedizened elderly men, potbellied or lean-shanked, one or the other always equally silly, he went far out of his way to avoid them.

"I do miss the children," Elinor said, "but not as much as I should. I wonder why?"

"We have not seen a great deal of them in late years," he said. "They lead their own lives early nowadays."

She said reflectively, "I think the real break began when we got the television and they took to spending their evenings in the television room without us."

"The other day," he said irrelevantly, only it was not irrelevant, because television men had been photographing the neo-Oriental crowds on the streets, "there was some sort of jamboree in New York, and I was ashamed to take Michael Cotman up the Avenue. I felt I couldn't explain."

"One of the animal orders?" she inquired, lifting an eyebrow.

"Something of the sort," he replied. Cotman was an English lawyer, representing his own firm in London, a middle-aged, good-natured man who asked no questions of anything he saw in the United States and expressed no opinions. His assumed acceptance of all he saw was alarming to any conservative American, such as William Asher considered himself to be. It could mean anything.

Herbert came to the door, immense in his white duck coat.

"Dinner is ready," he announced.

Elinor rose, putting out her hand for William's arm.

"Come, my love," she said. They marched into the dining room with playful formality behind Herbert's shielding back.

"I have always been so grateful," Elinor said, while William pushed her chair gently under her, "that you are exactly what you are."

He sat down, smiled at her above the bouillon which Herbert set before him, and meeting her eyes he saw there her love for him, shining like a mild and steady flame. A very lucky man, he thought, to live so well into middle age as he now was, and still see that light, which would last, he trusted, until the end. He bent his head and then in the continuing silence he heard quite clearly the sound of distant sobbing.

William put down his spoon.

"Can that be Jessica?" he inquired. Herbert had left the room.

"It is," Elinor said, and then she added with unusual sternness, "She should be ashamed to cry so loudly."

"But, my dear," he remonstrated.

"No, really, William," she broke in. "When a woman

28

cries out loud I can't feel sorry for her. It's indecent. What if we all did that? The world would be bedlam."

She rose and closing the window she cut off the sound. He did not answer. What did she mean by all women crying? He had never seen her shed a tear. He supposed that she had been too happy. He still could not fathom her entirely, even after twenty-five years of close living. It was simply one of those things she said, tossed off, meaningless except that when he pondered them, he felt them edged. He finished his soup in the artificial silence and Herbert came in and took the bowls away.

The bright autumn weather held. It was far too dry and the hardy chrysanthemums which he always enjoyed were small and dull, a disappointment, but not to be helped. He was very busy, for scandals had broken out in the city administration and he had the task of trying to decide whether he would defend the accused, and yet it was always difficult to decide whether he should, when it was obvious, as he thought it was, that the accused were guilty. The guilty had their rights, nevertheless, and it was a point nice to define, where their rights were fulfilled and where their guilt must stand.

He was face to face with the men, whom he was careful not to call the guilty, for that had not yet been proved, one morning in New York in late September. It was necessary for him to see them, in order, as they said, to get their side of the story which was, simply enough, that plenty of men had done what they had done and had not got into trouble and so in fairness, why should they?

He gazed into three fat smooth faces, glazed with years of good living and liquor, and tried not to recognize their racial origins, all different and yet all symbolic of the roots of evil in the political system of the greatest city in the world. Not that race or national origin had anything to do with it, he well knew, but the environment which society had forced upon the origins had a great deal to do with it. City slums, gang fights, prejudices and blows and finally crime had created the three he saw before him, whatever their racial origins. He felt remote and clean, a grey Vermont figure as he sat behind his desk and looked at them steadfastly.

"It all depends," he said, "upon what you want of me. If you will be content to have me fight for your right to plead your case, to be heard, to present every extenuating circumstance, that I can and will do. But if you expect me to prove you innocent, you will have to convince me first of your innocence."

The three fat faces looked blank. The big one coughed and spoke. "We know lawyers like you cost money and we'll pay." He had a strangely good accent, not an ignorant man, William decided, contemplating him with his usual high cool gaze.

"Certainly I expect to be paid for what I do," William agreed, "but I repeat my question—what do you want of me?"

The small fat one, the one in the middle, leaned forward coaxing. "Have a heart," he said in a husky pleading voice, a spoiled child voice, a babyish mouth, pouting and pretty. Somewhere along the way from the cradle his mother had yielded everything to the baby face, the pretty mouth. He was glad again that Elinor had been too intelligent to be a yielding mother. He had thought her sometimes harsh, but she had loved the children cleanly and without self-indulgence. Her honesty had remained inexorable.

"You do not convince me," William said coldly at last.

They had settled upon the defense, after he had spent the morning explaining to these three, who had never understood before, that innocence was a quality entirely apart from their rights as citizens. Guilty they might be, and he did not wish to know whether they were or not, for that was for the judge and the jury to decide, but they had their rights.

The fattest one, the swarthy, greasy, silent one, had given a retching sigh. "I guess it's the best we can do."

It was hard for them to believe that he could not be bought, coaxed, persuaded or in any way moved from his impregnable position. They accepted what he said because they trusted him and knew he was able but they could not understand him. That he did not refuse to defend their rights, that he did refuse to defend their actions, here was confusion. He saw it in their jowlish faces. They rose together, bewildered between humility and braggadocio, and left him cursing himself for a fool. Months of sifting evidence lay ahead of him, dividing strand from strand, protecting, in a sense, men whom he despised, and yet this was the honor of the law, before whom none was guilty until guilt had been proved. He had defended murderers up to the electric chair itself, and there he had left them, knowing his duty done.

He went home at the end of the week, feeling that he would have been exhausted except for the grimness of the task ahead of him. He could not afford weariness now for months to come, in the dissection of the underworld of this vast city which was to be his task. Thank God, he thought, for his peaceful distant home, for his quiet wife, for security of the heart.

Jessica opened the door when he came home, dimpling at the sight of him, pretty in a fresh blue uniform and white ruffled apron. There had been no more sobbing from upstairs and the wedding, he understood, was to be soon.

She took his hat and coat, and tempted as by a child

31

to a pleasant remark, he asked, "When is the great day, Jessica?"

Her brightness did not falter. "Next Saturday week, sir. It's Herbert's birthday."

"A very special celebration, eh?" His foot was on the bottom stair. Upstairs he heard Elinor singing as she busied herself somewhere.

"He says," Jessica agreed from the coat closet.

He went on up the stairs and at the landing, which turned sharply less than half way, he chanced to look down over the bannisters. There to his astonishment he saw Jessica again pausing in the east parlor on the way back to the kitchen. It was the third time, once when she was a child, once as a girl. Now she was a woman and again she seated herself in the rose velvet chair in front of the long oval mirror, and in the mirror he saw her reflected face, smiling, not indeed the bright childish smile he knew so well, but an affected grimace, as though she beheld in the glass a stranger. Her right hand caught up her short fair hair and held it on top of her head in a new coiffure and her left hand waved as though she held a fan. She spoke silent words, twisting her pretty mouth, and her large blue eyes were fixed in strange enchantment upon herself. What habit was this?

He was really startled now, and for a moment stood staring at her. Then deciding not to betray his observation, this time even to her, he tiptoed to his room, leaving her there with herself, a fancied self, a stranger certainly to him. Was this the way she always behaved when she thought no one was looking? When he and Elinor were away, when the house was empty, did she make free with any room she chose, imagining what she chose, forgetting her proper place as a servant? He was outraged at the possibility and closing the door of his room, he paused to consider whether it was his duty to tell Elinor at once.

The distant sound of her voice was still to be heard, her good contralto, a voice he had often thought might have been trained to rich quality. Again he decided against mentioning the matter. Elinor might take it far too seriously, and Jessica was so soon to leave the house forever. Bertha had decided that. Jessica was to go to the farmhouse and be a proper wife, and Bertha would have a place to spend her vacations, a place to live when she was too old to work. There was no use in making an upset these last few days.

He changed into his usual dark trousers and wine velvet jacket and then went to find Elinor, trying not to feel troubled. The singing had ceased, but he found her in the small linen room looking, so she explained, for a certain lace scarf which she wanted for the small mahogany chest in her bedroom. He stood waiting, enjoying her looks, and now glad he had not disturbed her calm. Whatever she had been doing in the day it must have been pleasant, for her face, expressive, mobile, was fresh and handsome. She had put on a silver grey teagown which he liked, and she wore at her bosom a pearl pink velvet rose. They embraced, and for once he wished that his home was not so far from New York. The hope that Elinor might be willing to come with him when he had to be in his city office, now that the children were grown, was not fulfilled. She disliked the city, and he continued his contriving of time, his arranged life, wherein the study he needed to make for his cases could be done in the Manchester office, or here at home, quiet days whose fruit, he hoped, was the soundness with which later he argued for his clients.

"It was cheerful to hear you singing when I came into the house," he said.

"That tune has caught itself in my mind all day," she

replied. "A tag end of that song we heard at the theater a month ago. But why was it in my mind?"

She did not expect an answer and he did not give one. She found the scarf and placed it and they went downstairs together. The living room was empty, the rose velvet chair was in its place, and the mirror reflected merely themselves, arm in arm.

The next morning Jessica waylaid him at the door to the library. He had brought home with him in the black leather briefcase a mass of documents, letters, newspaper clippings, material his junior partners had been collecting for him during the week, and now it remained for him to digest this until it was as familiar to him as the history of his own life. He had risen early, oppressed during his sleep by the faces of the three men whose rights he had chosen to defend.

"Please, sir," Jessica said.

William stopped to look at her sternly, mindful of yesterday. "Yes?"

Jessica twisted her apron with one hand and the other flew to her pink cheek. "Please, Mr. Asher, sir, don't think you must come to my wedding. I know Mrs. Asher will think so, because of my mother, but I don't mind a bit—indeed, sir, I'd rather you didn't."

He was impatient with her. "Yes? Oh well, I'll speak to Mrs. Asher about it. As a matter of fact, I shall be very busy about that time."

"And sir," she pleaded, for this was not all, as he could see, though puzzling enough, "could you not do one more thing? You are the kindest one in the house—yes, sir, I don't mean that the mistress isn't kind, but she's for my mother, if you know what I mean and I can't blame her for that, for Mother has been here so long and all, long before I was born, of course, but might I come back

34

afterwards, sir, and do my work here just as if I wasn't married?"

This was quite outside his province. He never meddled in the house, especially when the servants were really Winsten property, Herbert having come through Bertha, and Jessica belonging to Bertha. Besides, what about yesterday? That sort of thing could not go on unchecked.

Jessica saw his surprise, his doubt. Her violet eyes implored, lovely, yes, he saw unwillingly, with long amber lashes shades darker than her hair. Poor child—such beauty meaningless, he supposed.

Jessica hurried on. "If it isn't presuming, sir, this house is really my home." The violet eyes swept the handsome old rooms. "I can remember when I was such a small thing, really not more than three or four years old, I used to push open that door, sir," she pointed toward the pantry entrance into the hall, "and I'd stand there, pretending it was all mine. It was naughty but that's what I did. And when I was a bit bigger, more bold, I daresay, I used to come in when the family was away and my father out in the garden and Mother in the kitchen, and I'd sit down in that chair there"—it was the rose velvet chair—"and pull it up to the mirror and see myself here in the midst of the beautiful rooms, and I'd pretend again. Oh, I was naughty all right and that's why Mother sent me to the convent when I was only seven because she found me doing that and she said I was getting above myself. But it was only that I loved the house so much, and the family, and I still do and must always, because it's been my home, like."

He was astounded at all this and very uncomfortable indeed. Pretending it was all hers! Did she forget he had seen her at it himself? "Well, Jessica, I can speak to Mrs. Asher—"

"Oh, please, but not to tell her what I've said! For it

35

is presumptuous, I know that, and she might not understand, being one of the family, but you, sir—"

He was very unwilling to admit an understanding that Elinor did not share, especially to this girl who was so unsuitably a servant, for he guessed there were all sorts of delicacies and moods here which could not possibly do her any good, her station being what it was, not that he believed in station as any sort of permanence, but it took an energy he doubted she possessed to get out of the estate to which she was born.

"Well, Jessica," he said with determined coldness, "I will do the best I can, but if Mrs. Asher decides your mother would be too much hurt by our not coming to the wedding, you must forgive us if we are there. As to the rest of it, you'd better wait a bit after the wedding. It might come about quite naturally during the holidays, say, when the children are all home, that we'd need extra help, and we'd call on you."

She glowed far beyond the faint hope. "Oh, thank you, Mr. Asher." Her thin hands flew together.

"It's no promise, mind you," he told her.

"Oh, I'll understand," she breathed.

He went on toward the library and forgot her in the immensities of the city corruption. By the end of the day, when he remembered again, the incident seemed slight, not worth repeating to Elinor. He had learned long ago that the peace in a home is kept as much by forgetting as by remembering, and Elinor might be annoyed that Jessica had made so strange a request as to come back to work instead of staying at home, a request so calculated to annoy the far more important Bertha. Nevertheless, the forgetfulness was not so complete that, days later, when Elinor reminded him of the wedding he told her that he would not be able to go. This was true. Even had Jessica not spoken, he would have been hard put to it to be at home, certainly not at two o'clock.

"My dear," he said, "I cannot leave the city at all next week. I shall have to go in early Monday morning and you won't see me again until Friday or even Saturday. We shall be preparing our briefs, the other men cannot possibly do this without me, and I could scarcely attend the wedding even if it were Susan's."

"Bertha will be hurt," Elinor observed, "especially as the children aren't here, and the rest of my family is so scattered. My brothers and sisters are nomads—I don't know why. I hope the children won't be so. I suppose Cousin Emma will come."

"I am sorry you have a nomadic husband, too," he said lightly. It would have been easy to tell her now what Jessica had said, but it seemed not worth while, the mood of a servant girl, which it had only made him uncomfortable to share for a moment. He was glad that Jessica was going and he would not help her to return. He was not pleased to think that she considered this house, now his, as her home, even her spiritual home, so to speak.

Thus the wedding took place without him and when he came home late the Saturday after, tired and tense with the rising energy that he always felt when a major case proceeded towards its climax, he forgot that Jessica was gone. It was only when Bertha served the dinner alone that he remembered. He felt compelled to be kind.

"Well, Bertha, not a daughter lost—a son gained, eh? I am sorry I couldn't be at the wedding."

"Herbert will be back next week, sir," she replied. "I toldt him a week is plendy. Heinrich and me, we tookt only two dayss. But Herbert sayss the chicken haus shall get a new roof and he makes it in the honeymoon."

"Good," he said heartily, but somehow feeling it not good at all.

"The wedding," Elinor said when Bertha had left the room, "was really pitiful. There was nobody there except Herbert's brothers and sisters and Cousin Emma. Her chauffeur drove her from New York. It was sweet of her to come, but she kept saying afterwards in such a loud voice that she didn't like Herbert's looks."

"Did Cousin Emma go straight back?" he inquired, for conversation.

"No, she spent the night here, and I had to assure her that Herbert was really just the sort of person that Jessica needs. Jessica is rather flighty, William. You don't notice it, being away so much, but sometimes she is quite wearing. Well-trained servants should never impose their moods, my mother used always to say. Heinrich and Bertha never did. Heinrich might have, he was inclined to be the soft sentimental German type, but Bertha kept a firm hand. I know my father had only to look hard at Heinrich when he fumbled something and Bertha took over."

"How is Cousin Emma?" he asked, still in abstraction. He should really have spent Sunday in the city. The single witness upon whom much depended was under guard, but could the city be trusted?

"Fading," Elinor said gently and then she went on, "I often wonder what Cousin Emma has had out of life. She kept talking about Jessica as a little girl. It seems she took notice of her when she visited us. Still she likes to live in New York, 'the city of lonely women,' she calls it, where she can enjoy music and lectures and art. She is getting queer, I suppose, though so sweet."

"Queer?" he echoed.

Bertha was serving a delightful baked scrod.

"She leaned towards me the way she does," Elinor went on. "She tapped my wrist. 'I have a beautiful Turner painting,' she whispered. Now where could she get a Turner, William? They cost thousands. So I said, 'Have you, Cousin Emma?' And she laughed without making the slightest sound and went on. 'Yes, in the Frick gallery. I sit there every day for hours and enjoy it. Nobody knows it's mine, but it is. I own it—in here,' and she tapped her old caved-in bosom."

Elinor's father had made William one of the trustees of Cousin Emma's small inheritance. "I must look into that," he said, troubled. "It may be she is getting incompetent. She lives alone, doesn't she?"

"In that old hotel," Elinor said. "I'd go to see her oftener but it's such a distance."

He looked at her half humorously. "A distance I travel weekly in order to live with you."

She acknowledged this fondly. "Ah, I know! I ought to take the house in town that you wanted now that I don't have the children as an excuse. But I still hate the city."

He had accepted this years ago, when she declared that she could live nowhere but in Vermont. "Never mind, my dear," he said. "The roads are wonderful, the highways come almost to our door, and it is much easier than it used to be for me when the children were small. Then, too, I acknowledge that in this native air of ours my brain cells function well."

Nevertheless a few days later in a lull for new evidence he took an hour away from his city office and went to call upon Cousin Emma, his secretary having made the appointment.

He found her in a small overstuffed apartment, a lank agitated old lady, a tall figure draped in chiffon of a faded blue, the color of her eyes, and she was guarded by an elderly hotel maid, who opened the door and later brought in the heavy silver tea tray.

"It is very nice of you to come and see me, William,"

39

Cousin Emma said. "I hope there is nothing wrong with my affairs."

"Not at all," William replied, taking his seat opposite the yellow brocaded satin chair. Gas logs burned between, and there was a reek of gas in the air. He must speak to the superintendent. The kind old lady might be suffocated some night, accustomed to the atmosphere, as he could see, and every window shut. The gas logs looked old enough to fall apart. He went on.

"Elinor told me you had gone up for Jessica's wedding and I told myself it had been a long time since I came to see you—too long. After all, you are, in a manner of speaking, my ward, you know."

She gave him a sweet withered smile. "I am quite well, William. It was a jaunt for me to get up to Manchester for the wedding, but Bertha had written me about it and I felt some of the family should go. As it turned out, only Elinor and I were there. I remember Jessica so well before she went to the convent—such a beautiful little thing and so gifted. Really, William, it is a pity. I came upon her one day years ago, in the long east parlor. She was at the piano, singing very softly, touching the keys quite in harmony, and the most heavenly clear little voice. I ought to have taken her straight out of that house and educated her in music. But"—Cousin Emma leaned forward in her enthusiasm—"she paints equally well, or could have, if she had been taught. I remember once when she was home at Christmas she gave me a water color she had done for a present. She used to make little gifts for me because she knew I was fond of her and she gave them to me secretly. I found the water color rolled up and tied with a holly ribbon and hidden in my bureau drawer. I still have it somewhere—"

Her eyes grew vague, thinking where it could be.

"And that man," she said suddenly. "He is so very thick."

He knew she meant Herbert. "Nevertheless very stable, if solid," he suggested.

"Oh, I don't know," Cousin Emma said, suddenly distracted. She wrung her long thin hands. "Do you want some more tea, William?"

"One more cup," he said to please her. "It is delicious tea."

She was very pleased. "Oh, do you like it? It is special but so few people would know. I get it from a Chinese shop, such a delightful place. I imagine, you know, William, that I am travelling quite around the world, all the while I am living here in New York. The other day I found a real Italian fiesta, two streets downtown shut off from traffic, and there were hundreds of lights festooned across them and the quaintest bazaar going on. I had gone to buy this very tea when your secretary telephoned you were coming. I often wish I had brought Jessica here with me, William. I believe she would have been glad to come. You know, Bertha was too strict with that little child. I used to see her snatching her by the arm. It wasn't wrong for the little thing to steal about those big empty rooms. Nobody knew except me, really. Everybody else was so busy."

"Yet Bertha loves Jessica very much," he suggested, without telling her what he thought of Jessica's behavior.

Cousin Emma made a grimace of distaste. "Oh, don't talk to me about love, please, William. It's made such an excuse. That is the way my own sister Jessica used to begin—'You know I love you, Emma, but—'"

She laughed shrilly. Elinor's mother was a woman gentle and beloved, William believed, except by Cousin Emma.

Yet he could detect no signs of madness in the old lady.

41

She had always been wilful, difficult, frustrated he supposed because she had never married, although she had had chances enough, he had been told, and he did not know why she had not accepted any of them. So far as he knew, there had never been a tragedy. He rose after a third cup of tea, relieved that no new problem must confront him just now.

"You are going to be quite rich this year, Cousin Emma," he said by way of parting cheer. "Your stocks are rising. Dividends are inevitable."

But she was not cheered. "Oh, don't speak of that," she cried. "It's only this horrible talk of another war. I'd rather go to the poorhouse than get rich from it." She fumbled for a bit of ragged newspaper in her black velvet handbag hanging from her wrist and put up her pince-nez to her eyes. "Making atomic bombs!" She put down the glass and gazed at him with reproach. "And you talk to me about dividends!"

"Forgive me," he said contritely. "I'd forgotten how you follow the news."

"If I weren't so old," she said dramatically, "I'd pour out my blood. But they don't want it. It's too old. Why not? Does blood change?" She held out her withered right arm, the lace sleeve falling back.

"I suppose it does," he said. "I suppose the doctors know."

She let the arm drop upon her knee. "I am very glad I never married. I thank God I never had a son. I couldn't have taken the suffering now." She leaned forward. "What are you doing about your sons?"

"They will have to do what other young men do," William replied.

"There, you see," she exclaimed. "They are in for a lot of suffering, and you, too. That is what marriage brings. I do wish I had told Jessica to come here. I didn't think of it, not until I saw her standing up by that thick fellow. Bertha is thick, too. I don't know why I didn't command Jessica to come and live with me. She could have gone to the galleries with me. I have a wonderful Turner there— quite my own, although nobody knows."

Was this the tinge of madness? No, he saw nothing but the old wilfulness. Cousin Emma was entirely sane, merely wilful in her fancy, as she had always been, delighting to bewilder.

"That is pleasant," he said. "Now I must be going, Cousin Emma. A most delicious tea—I shall have to tell Elinor."

He pressed her long bony old hand, and went away. Nothing here but the irresponsibility of age, he thought, the determination not to be what people, he or anyone else, expected. It would have been very bad for Jessica to live alone with this, much better, indeed, for her to tread the ordinary path of woman, to marry, to have a home of her own and childen in due time. That way lay health and sanity and companionship. For there was a companionship, he felt sure, in the mere sharing of a common life beneath one roof. Love was the glory of a marriage, the cup running over, but marriage itself was the necessity. He doubted the enthusiasm of Cousin Emma, he doubted the talents that she saw in Jessica, there was nothing to warrant such gifts in the stodgy heritage of Bertha and Heinrich. The nuns perhaps had given her taste, but it might be forgotten, if it still existed, in the growing of her normal life. He dismissed Jessica, somewhat impatient that quite without his will or interest, she appeared so often and so irrelevantly in his life.

AT CHRISTMAS time Susan brought home a dog. William, riding in the car half asleep with fatigue, his eyes closed behind Herbert's stolid back, opened them to see his daughter in the frosty dusk. She was waiting for him at the gate, between the elm trees. He saw her short strong figure, swathed in a white fur jacket, and then he saw a huge black dog of an unknown breed, pulling savagely at a leather lead she had wrapped about her right hand. He stopped the car and opened the window.

"What's that animal?" he shouted.

"It's not an animal, it's a dog," she cried back at him. "His name is Pirate!"

"I can't get out," he grumbled. "I can't ask you in. He looks as though he'd chew one up."

"He's only young," she retorted, struggling against the plunging beast, now furiously barking at the car, at the night, at everything, William thought, most of all at him.

"Whatever possessed you to bring him home?" He was compelled to shout because the dog had a deep bass roar that echoed through the woods.

"He's immense," she cried. "He eats two pounds of meat at a meal!"

"Two pounds! He looks as though he'd think nothing of fifty!" William retorted.

He could not get near her and he called gloomily

through the half darkness, "I'll see you later when I'm safe in the house. You don't bring him in, I hope."

"He insists on it," Susan screamed and braced herself against a tree.

"Horrible," William muttered and closed the window. "Go on, Herbert. The night air is cold."

To all this Herbert had made no remark. He seldom spoke unless spoken to and this, William thought, was his greatest virtue. Secretly he was astonished at other changes in Herbert during the last weeks since the wedding. Always a cautious and even slow driver, Herbert had begun in a stealthy fashion to speed. Tonight he had crept out of the city at a sober rate, and as he approached the parkways he had properly increased his speed. Nevertheless after a while William had stirred from a half doze, aware of a faint giddiness, and peering into the front seat he saw the speedometer edging eighty.

"Good God, Herbert!" he cried sharply.

Herbert gave a violent start and the car swerved dangerously close to the other lane.

"Keep your eyes on the road," William had shouted. That was another folly the man had. When addressed he would turn his head, leaving the car to manage for itself. "You'll get arrested!"

Herbert dropped so suddenly to fifty that the car seemed to stop with a jerk. "Sorry, sir. My mind was wanderin'."

"Never let your mind wander on the road," William said sternly, and he did not doze again for an hour.

Now entering the house he kissed Elinor at the door and began to complain. "Herbert very nearly had an accident this afternoon. He was driving at eighty miles an hour."

Elinor replied with proper concern, "I can't imagine it."

45

"He was," William insisted. "I spoke to him and he said his mind was wandering."

The door to the pantry opened and to his astonishment he saw Jessica come in, dressed in a blue cotton uniform and ruffled white apron. She dimpled at his surprise as she took his coat and hat. "It's only for the holidays, sir, but it will give me a bit of change."

He remembered now that he had said something about this, and his exacting conscience was roused. "Look here, I had nothing to do with it. In fact, I forgot all about it. You'll have to thank Mrs. Asher."

Elinor stood waiting, looking, he thought, somewhat aloof.

"It's lovely being back, madame," Jessica said with a strange pleading urgency. "Indeed I do thank you."

"It will be a help to have you here while the children are at home," Elinor said. Her voice was cool and kind.

William turned to the stairs and felt her hand tucked in his elbow. They mounted the steps together and in silence. When they reached the upstairs sitting room they shared, the two bedrooms opening from it, she sat down. This was a pleasant room furnished in the opulent but unadorned style which he liked and which seemed native to the Winstens. There was no bric-a-brac. There were no ruffles or dust catchers of any sort. The curtains were a plain clear blue satin, very heavy, and the old Persian carpet caught the same blue in its multifold regular pattern. Blue became his wife, her eyes very blue under her silver blonde hair. He sat down to fill his pipe before undertaking the task of washing and changing. The house was still, but from outdoors he could hear the harsh bass roar of the dog's barking.

"Is Winsten's family here yet?" he asked.

"Madge telephoned that they couldn't make it until tomorrow," Elinor replied. "Edwin came, but he went out at once to see Vera. Susan arrived on schedule, with a young man and a dog."

"I saw the dog," he replied. "A vile beast."

"You can't say that publicly," she retorted. "The young man gave it to her."

"Where is he?"

"Asleep, I believe. He ate a great deal of cake and a plateful of sandwiches, declined tea and drank two high-balls and then said he was sleepy."

"Have we seen him before?" William inquired.

"No, dear," Elinor replied. "He's quite new."

"What's he like?"

Elinor considered. "A good deal like the dog—large, rough, a plain family, I judge—oh, very plain—but Susan tells me the girls think he's wonderful."

This made him think of something. "Why is it this generation of young females likes them in the rough? If I remember, you used to keep me right up to the mark. Now the more the young men talk out of the corner of their mouths, swear, sprawl, generally act like gangsters, the more girls like them."

Elinor considered this. She sat gracefully composed, a figure as aristocratic as could be designed, perhaps, in a democracy as new as America, her narrow feet, encased in silver slippers, crossed beneath her long skirt of fine black lace over some sort of a cherry-colored stuff, satin, he supposed, since it did not rustle. She disliked rustling garments.

"I don't know," she said thoughtfully. "I do know that I detest Susan's young men. I only pray that she does not marry any of the ones we have seen."

"Vera, on the other hand—" he said, thinking of Edwin.

"Oh, Vera, of course, would be wonderful," Elinor said at once. Then hesitating, reluctant, she went on, "I have a mad sort of notion that I ought not to put into words."

"Do," he urged. "Between us, we have said a number of mad things."

"I wonder if Jessica has some ridiculous notion about Edwin?"

He was startled indeed. "Now that really is mad," he said. "Jessica, trained by Bertha, could scarcely so forget herself! Besides, Edwin is only a kid—what's Jessica?"

"Twenty-four—"

"Well, then twenty-one to twenty-four."

"Edwin is very handsome, and I would feel happier," she went on, "if Jessica were not so pretty—oh, so what people used to call refined, you know—delicate, perhaps, and certainly far too sensitive for a servant."

"What did you see?" he asked, unwillingly troubled.

"Jessica laughing, her hands on Edwin's shoulders, and he looking down, blushing—"

He was so much upset by this that he felt he ought to tell her something which until now had not had a shape definite enough for words, not the posturing before the mirror, but something he had not expressed even to himself.

"You know," he said with uneasy reluctance, "Jessica has a very odd way with any man."

She looked at him with eyes suddenly direct. "What do you mean, William?"

He did not know how to answer. Put into words, it seemed too much beyond the truth. He laughed but with constraint. "There, I don't know what I mean. When I try to explain, the thing escapes me. Perhaps it's a way she has of looking coaxing or wistful. It has always made me uncomfortable and I escape immediately. I'm sure she's too innocent to know how she looks."

"No woman is so innocent," Elinor said, quite without rancor, he decided, after he had stared at her.

"We are born wise," she said, now, he believed, half

48

teasing him. "It's our only escape to freedom. The more enslaved women are, the more wise we become."

"You aren't enslaved," he declared.

"Then I am not wise?" she demanded.

She had slipped into the remoteness where sometimes she lived for days at a time. He knew the mood so well, and long ago he had learned merely to smile, to accept, and if possible to love her more while he waited. He replied, "Though I am a lawyer considered famous in a mild way I know better than to let you engage me and I shall go and wash the city from me and change into something comfortable. As for Jessica and Edwin, no, I will not believe it, but I shall keep my eyes open."

"It reassures me," Elinor said, "to have you say that even you feel Jessica makes a special approach. So long as it is to all men, my dear—"

"Make the best of it," he replied tranquilly. He felt too tired to be serious.

The trial in the city was not going well. That star witness, that treasure store of evil knowledge, had been allowed to escape long enough to be bribed by the devil only knew what, so that he had refused to divulge what he had promised to tell and he was now behind prison bars where he was entirely safe, but entirely useless. The city would have to pay for a long renewed examination of facts hidden inside that solid skull to which there was no combination known that might force the lock and lift the lid.

He forgot his family while he bathed and shaved again, for his beard grew apparently upon city soot and dust so that he must needs shave at night as well as morning if he was to present a cheek smooth enough at bedtime to tempt Elinor's lips. Then he heard a door open and slam shut again and a clatter upon the stairs such as neither of his two sons had made even in their liveliest childhood.

It was, he knew at once, Susan's young man, the Pirate, he thought, the giver of the dog so like him that even Elinor the merciful, the tolerant, the more than kind, saw the resemblance.

The resemblance was plain enough to him, too, when later he entered the east parlor. The dog was lying on the rug before the fire, where no dog had ever lain, for William was not a lover of dogs and when the children had clamored for those animals in their childhood he had permitted cocker spaniels but only outdoors. He was sensitive to the smell of dog and the room was full of it.

"Susan," he began, impetuous with horror, seeing his daughter vaguely in a yellow frock billowing about her slender waist and brown shoulders.

"I know, Dad," she said, "but Pete says that Pirate simply has to be indoors or he'll howl all night."

An immense young man rose out of his own leather chair, a length of male flesh and bone, hollow eyes pitch black under heavy black brows and stiff black hair surely never brushed nor combed and needing to be cut. The fellow wore a dark suit of some sort, but the coat was carelessly unbuttoned over a rumpled blue shirt in which he had undoubtedly slept. His high cheek bones were red, his red ears were too big and the hand which he now thrust out briskly was enormous and hairy.

"Mr. Asher?" he bellowed.

"I presume," Susan said pertly. "Don't you know the proper address, Pete? Dad, he's Peter Dobbs."

But Pete had never heard of Livingstone in Africa, and the mild joke escaped him.

"I'm pleased to meet you," he said with a loose southern accent. "I've heard a lot about you. I been readin' the papers since I got to know Susan. I really admire the way you been cuttin' circles round the gangsters. Too bad they let Bergman escape, if you call it that now he's in jail."

The dog leaped up and braced his forefeet. The thick black hair on its back rose at the sight of William. He growled like a bass drum.

"Shut up, Pirate," Pete said carelessly. "Lie down, dawg! He's just not used to you all yet."

"I doubt that I shall ever be used to him," William said with tartness.

"I reckon you will," Pete said comfortably. He folded himself in the leather chair again.

"Pete, get up," Susan said imperiously. "That's my father's chair."

"Don't disturb yourself," William said with bitter courtesy.

"Get up, I tell you," Susan repeated.

Pete got up, amiable, to take another chair. "I don't care wheah I sit, just so the chair's big enough. I don't like anything tight."

"Sit down, Dad," Susan commanded. "He really doesn't care. He's good-natured but you have to speak plainly to him. He doesn't understand anything else. It makes him awfully easy to get on with."

She spoke these outrageous words in her calm contralto, a pretty voice, a soft resonant sweetness under its attempted curtness. William sat down, feeling helpless. The huge dog collapsed on the rug again and he found himself staring into its furious eyes. They were fixed upon him under lowering brows, red in the reflected light of the fire.

"That dog looks bad tempered," he said, somewhat sourly. Privately he made up his mind that he would speak to Susan alone at the first moment and command her to remove this wild animal from his hearth.

"He ain't bad tempered," Pete said. "He just looks thataway—cain't help it."

"Like you," Susan said without a smile.

Pete guffawed in admiration. "You sure have a mean little tongue! Some day when you stick it out at me I'm goin' to take out mah knife like this"—he took a large clasp knife from his pocket, and flipped open the blade— "and I'm goin' to cut that little tongue right off and give it to Pirate to eat up."

William listened to this in horror. He felt unable to cope with it. Gangsters in a courtroom in a vast wicked city were all very well, but he did not expect to find a monster in his own house.

"Where is your mother?" he asked Susan. "Tell her I'd like my dinner."

"We are waiting for Edwin," Susan replied without stirring. "Mother said he telephoned at the last minute that he was bringing Vera to dinner."

Commotion in the hall signified Edwin's arrival and a moment later they came in, his tall younger son, blond as all the Winstens were, and with him the equally tall Vermont girl, the daughter of the local banker, Vera Bates, a silver birch of a girl, severely beautiful, whose lips, though thin and straightly cut, were tender.

He rose gallantly, this was his kind of a girl, a reassuring youthful creature whom he would delight to welcome into his house and family. The dog rose again to growl, but Vera stooped and smoothed down its rising scruff and the belly growl subsided. The beast snorted and sank down again.

"Your inestimable charm," William said, and putting out his hand, he felt her cool palm against his.

"Good evening, Mr. Asher," she said very correctly.

"Good evening, my dear," he replied, "and you, Edwin, are looking very well, my son."

He felt happy again. There were also these young people, and the soundness of a great country was that, however unpleasant parts of it were, and however uncouth certain sections undoubtedly were, there were to be found elsewhere one's own kind, those of whom he could be proud.

He felt mildly sorry for Pete, the uncouth and unpleasant, and when they were all seated he leaned toward him.

"What sort of dog—"

At this moment Elinor came in from somewhere, the pantry perhaps, for she was concerned about her table, fastidious over the serving of food. She pressed Vera's hand gently and sat down in the chair left empty for her, the rose velvet. William rose and pushed the small needlepoint footstool toward it.

"Thank you, dear," she said.

He sat down then and surveyed his family with loving care and found them good, and feeling sorry again for Pete, whom he could never count among them, he leaned once more toward that uncouth young man who had remained sprawled in amiable silence.

"What sort of dog is Pirate?" he inquired, not knowing what conversation could be made that would include this incongruous pair.

"He ain't any sort of dawg," Pete replied without embarrassment. "He's just a mungrel. We got plenty of dawgs like that in my dad's place. I took to Pirate because he's big. He's smart, too. He kin learn. He'll do anything I say. Hyeah, Pirate—"

Pete snapped his fingers and the dog sprang up bristling, its glittering eyes alert, its sharp ears cocked.

"If I told him, he'd spring at anybody in this room," Pete said proudly.

"Oh—"

The half strangled cry came from the doorway and they turned their heads simultaneously to see who had made that cry, so strange, so stifled. It was Jessica. She had come to announce dinner, and now, facing the dog, she stared at it in terror, her hands knotted at her throat. The dog rose stealthily to its feet, its eyes fixed upon her.

"Lie down, dawg," Pete commanded.

"Jessica," Elinor said, warning.

"Yes, madame." The hands dropped. "I—dinner is served, please."

Jessica disappeared. They rose and the dog did not move.

"Come here, Pirate," Pete commanded.

The dog followed him into the dining room.

"Lie down there," Pete commanded, pointing to the spot beside the closed French doors.

The dog hesitated.

"Lie down, I say!" Pete bawled.

The dog collapsed heavily and Pete sat down and grinned at them all. "Like I said, he'll do anything I tell him."

Jessica did not come in again. Herbert served the dinner, rather better, William noticed, than usual, and paying no attention to the dog, who growled every time he came in until Pete yelled at it. It was true. The dog obeyed.

"You'll have to teach me your magic," Susan said to Pete. They sat side by side and the dog lay on the carpet behind them.

"No magic," the young man replied. He was comfortably ladling food into his mouth with a strange combination of knife and fork working together as a conveyor. "He listens to one person at a time, 'at's all. Whichever person he belongs to, 'at's the one he listens to."

54

"How will he know he belongs to me?" Susan asked. "When I'm gone, he'll turn to you."

William heard this with alarm. "You aren't leaving the dog here!"

Pete lifted his huge head from his plate. "Susan's Christmas present," he explained.

"Oh, no!" Elinor cried.

Edwin lifted his handsome eyebrows at Vera, who answered by the slightest drop of her eyelids. Neither spoke.

Susan turned impetuously upon her mother. "He won't bother you, I shall take him back to college. The charwoman says he may stay with her if they won't let me keep him at the dormitory."

Elinor did not reply. Long ago she and William had agreed that not at the family table would they contend with their young, and certainly not, her firm face declared, before this stranger named Pete.

Her eyes met William's down the length of the table and he responded at once. "The weatherman predicts a white Christmas," he said with proper pleasantness. "I hope so, for Winsten's children will enjoy the snow so much."

"I'll have to get out the old sleds," Edwin suggested. Edwin always joined loyally in any necessary turn in the conversation.

"Do," Elinor said heroically. "We haven't used them for so long. It will be something new for the children to have a white Christmas. They were too small two years ago to remember. I don't believe that even little Billy can remember that far back, do you, William?"

"Certainly not," he replied. And behind the loyal conversation he was thinking that tomorrow the unspeakable Pete would be gone. What was the fellow's last name?

55

He had forgotten—not that it mattered! And as soon as he was gone he would command Susan to put the dog outdoors where it belonged.

Pete went in the early morning, flinging himself tousled into a car so old that nothing like it could be seen, William felt sure, outside the circle of the Ozarks. He surmised that under the wrinkled top coat and the same suit of yesterday Pete might still be wearing his pajamas. He watched all this from his bedroom window, wakened by the noise, but prudently not appearing until this voice in his house was gone. Susan he now saw come flying out of the door when Pete started the engine into a gasping roar of noise and smoke. She was frankly in her red wool dressing gown, a scarlet figure, her dark hair down her back, surprisingly long since last spring when she had decided to let it grow. William closed his eyes lest he see his beloved daughter kiss the unshaved and altogether repellent young male in the driver's seat, and then he opened them quickly in the hope that he could see for himself this was not to happen. It did not. Pete reached out a long arm from which a pajama sleeve could be seen distinctly from underneath the top coat, he squeezed Susan hard enough to make her shoulders disappear, but there was no kiss.

"Thank heaven," William breathed, and climbed back into bed to sleep for another hour.

Sleep was impossible, he quickly discovered. He had ordered Herbert last night when he went to bed that as soon as Pete left the dog was to be put outside, and Herbert now obeyed. The creature was asleep on the hearth rug again and Herbert went in masterfully and seized its collar. He was a man brutishly strong and the dog felt himself lifted up and half choked. He growled and could make no sound. The man was astride his back dragging him as he walked. A moment later the dog felt itself pushed through the door into the cold and the door was locked upon him. It flung its body against the door, bellowing, and this was the noise that William now heard, the uproar, the howls of a wild animal, and then he heard the dreadful sound of clawing upon the oaken front door, the pride of the house, the door so old that tradition said it had come from a massive oak upon the mountain side, already hundreds of years old when the Winsten family settled here in Vermont. He leaped out of bed, hastened into his wool dressing gown and met Elinor and Susan upon the stair, Herbert and Jessica converging upon them from the pantry and Bertha panting behind from the kitchen. William threw the door open and the dog hurled itself into the house.

"Absolutely this will not do!" William shouted. He turned on Susan, his pale eyes so furious that for the first time in her life he saw she was afraid of him. He took advantage of her astonished terror. "I will not have that dog in the house." He shouted in a way that surprised himself. "Get the beast out and keep it out."

Susan ran into the east parlor. The dog was on the hearth rug again, its enormous body pressed down, immobile with determination, its head on its great paws, seemingly docile, but its eyes were baleful as he glared at them all.

"Pirate." Susan fell on her knees beside him. "Good dog, Pirate."

The dog lifted its head at her and bared its teeth.

"Susan, come away," Elinor cried. "It's dangerous. Oh, what shall we do, and the children due in less than an hour?"

It was true. Winsten's train would arrive before nine o'clock and it was nearly half past eight.

"I shall send it away," William said firmly.

Susan screamed at him. "I won't have him killed! He's only strange. He knows Pete has left him. He's frightened of me because I'm strange to him, too, now that Pete isn't here. He's always seen us together."

"The dog can't stay here," William said, inflexible, but his heart, to his own disgust, began to melt in him. There were actually tears in his child's brown eyes.

"Oh dear, oh dear," Elinor murmured.

It was Jessica who now surprised them all, Jessica who was always so timid. She stepped forward from the rank of servants where she stood between Herbert and Bertha and she said quite clearly, "I'll take the dog, Miss Susan. I'll take it home. I've changed my mind, please, about staying. Mother can manage." She looked from one surprised face to the other, and fastened on William. "Please, sir, it's that I don't feel quite well, all of a sudden. Herbert didn't want me to come in the first place—he said it would upset me and it has somehow. But we could do with a watch dog. The house is so lonely. I'm often quite frightened. I daresay it will get used to me when it's alone with me there."

Was this not the solution, with the train time so near? They looked at each other uncertainly. Herbert did not speak.

Elinor turned to Bertha. "Can you really manage?" She saw that Jessica meant to leave at once, only why, when she had begged so earnestly . . . ?

"Herbert helps me," Bertha said.

"Of course you may all go home after the dinner is served tomorrow," Elinor said.

"*Ya, gewiss*," Bertha agreed.

So it was done. Once more Herbert attacked the dog. He flung one leg over the dog's back and seized the neck with such strangling force that the creature could not turn its head, could scarcely breathe, its choking a mere guttural mutter in the throat. Herbert dragged the dog out between his clenched knees.

William opened the front door and they all stood watching the man clutching the dog, mastering it by a force as brutal as its own, until they reached the old Packard taxicab which was Herbert's private conveyance. He lifted one hand to open the door, and the dog, loosened, snarled and turned his head enough to snatch the man's arm. Herbert kicked the dog's belly and in a rage he lifted the animal with his hands and one knee, flung it into the vehicle and shut the door.

"I won't come in the house," he called. "My arm is drippin' blood."

"You must go to the doctor," Elinor called back.

"How can Jessica drive with that beast?" William shouted.

"She's safe enough in the front—there's a thick glass between. And I don't need no doctor. The dog's not mad —only mean."

They stepped back into the house and through the window William watched the dog flinging itself against the doors and the glass, barking in a frenzy and then howling long screams of fury. In a few minutes Jessica came from the back door, neat in her long blue cloth coat fitting her slender figure, a little blue hat close to her head, looking as usual so unlike what she was, a servant. Without a glance at the dog she climbed into the closed off front seat and drove away.

It was over, the house was restored to decency and Christmas peace. William went upstairs and bathed and dressed and came down again shaved, composed enough for the day. Elinor and Susan were already in the dining room, waiting for him.

"Where is Edwin?" he asked. He pushed Elinor's chair

in behind her, a habit so ingrained that he no longer noticed what he did.

"Would you believe that he is still asleep?" Elinor replied.

"I'm glad he is. I wish I were," William grumbled. "What a way to begin Christmas Eve!"

Susan, he was glad to notice, was entirely subdued. She had on some sort of negligee, a rose-colored wool. He disliked negligees at breakfast, but he did not mention it, since of course she knew it. She was drinking her orange juice slowly, as though it were hard to swallow, and she looked pale.

Herbert came in with the coffee. Bertha had bandaged his wrist neatly.

"I don't see how Jessica can possibly manage that dog when she gets home alone," William said.

"I told her to leave him be, Mr. Asher, sir," Herbert said. "I told her to leave him stay in the back of the car until he was starved quiet. When he's weakened enough, I'll handle him. I'll teach him who's master."

Susan lifted her head for protest but William met her eyes sharply and at once. Their gaze was a clash, he did not yield, and her eyelids drooped.

"A very good idea, Herbert," William said.

"Thank you, sir," Herbert replied and poured a cup full of coffee.

THERE was enough going on in the world outside his family, William Asher told himself somewhat sourly one April evening, while he knotted his tie in front of the mirror in his dressing room, without having something going on again in his own family. He had the same feeling of resentment that he remembered having when he was a boy, more than a boy really, quarreling with his own father in a subterranean fashion, because he wanted to stop being merely summer people, and become bonafide citizens of Manchester, in order that he might see Elinor every day. He was then learning to play the piano, had been learning for some years, and played well enough to accompany Elinor while she sang, unless she chose something difficult out of German opera, which he did not feel suited her voice, even then. She had learned better as time went on, and he still enjoyed playing her accompaniments, though of course when they married and had the children that sort of thing had to wait. One of the pleasures of having the children out of the house at last was that Elinor and he had begun music again and he was delighted to find that his fingers were still nimble and her voice still lovely, though much lower in register than it had been when she was young. And again he remembered, that the summer before they were married, he had a strange infection in the palm of his hand, a swelling from within, there being no sign whatever on the surface skin, but simply first a soreness that mounted in a few days to a deep-seated agony centered in his hand but pervading his whole being. The fury of it was that he and Elinor were to perform at the summer concert, the big affair of the season, and he could not do his part, and in addition to his aching, throbbing palm, he had to see her on the platform at the town hall with another accompanist, a man older than he by four or five years and the personification of his intense jealousy for years thereafter, even when he and Elinor were married. Why not say what was true, staring at his own face here in the mirror, that he was still jealous in a strange silly way of Lorenzo Marquis? Marquis had continued as one of the summer people, and every year William had to endure the man's complacency about his own success. Marquis was by now several times a millionaire and had been deeply insulting the last time he came to dinner, he and his fancy third wife.

"Well, the house looks exactly as it used to," he said, and Elinor had replied somewhat tartly, "That is why we like it," which would have been well enough except that then Marquis said, "I like you—you haven't changed, either. William must be easy to live with," and then with a coarse look of admiration at the blonde young girl he had recently married he had said, "I seem to go through 'em fast, don't I, Tootles?" Tootles had merely smiled. She was a sleepy beauty, not needing to speak.

That early summer William had been the more angry because the swelling in his hand had come from within. It was not a wound, he had not fallen and cut his hand, he had not misused a tool, no knife had slipped. Simply from within himself somewhere had come this senseless painful infection which had robbed him of joy with Elinor.

Now in April, years later, he remembered his hand because he and Elinor were planning an Easter vacation to Atlantic City, where the sun was said to shine at this season, and he felt, as he had felt long ago, that something was wrong within him. Certainly the sun did not shine in Vermont. The persistent grey of the sky above his house had got him on edge. He longed to see the hard clear blue of a sea still cold, a clear blue sky and clouds, a clean chill wind, people in bright garments of spring, pacing the boardwalks, an Easter crowd.

He needed the change after a hard winter in which there had been weeks when he could not come home at all. And while this was going on, the scandal in the city now growing deeper until he was compelled to probe into the very sewers of humanity where life was horrible in its fertility, its growth, its vitality consuming the healthy life of the innocent, a cancer fastened upon the corporate frame, while all this was going on until he was sick to the core, something of the same sort was taking place far away in what he had always liked to think was the singularly pure and innocent state of Vermont, in the sacred spot which belonged to him and to Elinor, in his own home.

The disturbance centered ridiculously about the black dog, the enormous animal which Jessica had taken home with her on Christmas Eve. He had not thought of the beast again, and the holidays had been delightful, the snow had come, and for the first time, he recalled, he had enjoyed the pleasures of being a grandfather. Until now he had been ashamed that he somewhat resented at his youthful age the fact of a third generation already springing up around him. He had married early and so had Winsten, and Madge had been quite willing to have children at once, in the shameless fashion young women did these days. When he and Elinor were married the prompt

arrival of Winsten a bare twelve months after the cere-
mony had been a source of embarrassment to the whole
family, implying, quite unjustly, that he, William Asher,
as correct a young man then as ever lived, was a brute
of unleashed passions. Winsten and Madge, on the contrary, had been proud of their early marriage and had
been only the more so when less than a year later a boy
was born. At Christmas Madge announced herself again
pregnant, and quite unnecessarily, to every one who came
into the house.

"Yes, yes," she had cried, her round face, pink and
white, all laughter. "Isn't it wonderful? In July, the
twelfth—" There it was again, she named the very day,
implying a dreadful planning, inviting the prurient to
imagine the very night—or day for that matter, for he
had once seen something here in this house which revealed to him that Winsten did not wait decently until
night, but if he felt impelled, simply—

He turned away from the mirror where he had been
standing. At any rate, the children had been beautiful
in the Christmas snow, the boy in his scarlet coat and
leggings, and the little girl, still a baby and scarcely
able to stagger, in her bright blue costume and the little
white fur tippet she was so proud of, her eyes blue as
bits of sky when she stood up on a snow bank, outlined
against the sky itself. He had understood then something of the wonder of continuing human life, the beauty
of it in health and goodness here in his home, in blessed
contrast to the spawn of city filth. He would at least keep
his own in health and goodness, and if every man did
as well, corruption would die.

Yet a corruption had appeared here in his own house,
an infection from within, with which it seemed he had
nothing to do, and yet which could and did bring unease
to the whole.

He frowned, put on his coat, and went downstairs to dinner. A pleasant air of spring pervaded the rooms, although it was far too cold to open the windows, and there was as usual a fire burning upon the hearth. But Elinor had put early daffodils in bowls upon the table, and she wore a taffeta dress of April green, not new, he recognized, but still too cool for winter and therefore it was spring. She sat down, he pushed her chair under her, and took his own place. There were daffodils between them, very low in a silver dish, so that he could see her face. There it was, the remote look, the wistful distance, her cheeks a trifle pale, and her mouth red only because she had made it so. Something was wrong, but he delayed facing it. He could have his dinner first. He had planned to tell her the exasperations of his own week, for he could not come home except on Friday nights, as this was, and he must be back in the city by Tuesday morning.

"When this dirty business is over," he said somewhat harshly while Herbert served the soup in small broth bowls, "I shall take a month off and not go near the city. I am glad we have the few days next week at the sea."

The plan was that Elinor should meet him and they would leave the city together, so that actually it would be two weeks and perhaps more before they were home together again. He would miss her until then, but these were the last crowded years before his retirement. He had set that year for himself. After it he would be on call as a consultant for difficult cases, but he would do no more of the frontal attack that he was doing now. Younger men, perhaps Edwin, who had decided suddenly to be a lawyer, would take his place. But he would not take Edwin into the firm until he had proved himself in another. No nepotism—he loved his family too well, he was jealous for them, nothing must assail his children before each attained the top, alone. Marquis had ruined his only son, the boy was a man of twenty-five, still living on his father's absurd allowance, five thousand a month, pretending to write a play, a book, something. Marquis had provided a salary for him for years on his own radio station, but the boy did not know it. That had to stop when the employees had revolted.

"I don't know whether I ought to leave home just now," Elinor said.

"Why?" he demanded.

"I don't like the way Susan is behaving," Elinor said.

Her eyebrows lifted. Herbert was in the room. He had gained weight absurdly during the last few months, and his house coat was so tight that he was breathing in short gasps loud enough to be heard.

William noticed it and smiled slightly. "Looks like marriage agrees with you, Herbert," he said, helping himself to lamb roast.

Herbert, were he not addressed, could maintain silence for days on end, but a friendly comment could unlock the sealed gates within him. He stepped back, set the meat platter upon the silver trivet on the buffet and spoke, first coughing behind his thick right hand.

"Jessica ain't going so good," he said in his rather thin voice.

"No?" William said. It had been a mistake to notice Herbert.

"I was thinkin'," Herbert said, lowering his voice, "that I would like to have a talk with you and Mrs. Asher tonight, if you have the time."

William inquired of Elinor silently by a look of secret exasperation, conveyed by his uplifted eyebrows.

"Oh, certainly," she said, "as soon as dinner is over, Herbert, while we are having our coffee. Then you won't

66

be so late getting home. Jessica must feel nervous there alone at night until you come."

"She has the dog," Herbert said.

No more was said, they finished their dinner and withdrew to the living room. There comfortably seated William sighed. "I wish we needn't go through with this. Have you any idea—"

Elinor interrupted. "I know that things haven't been right since Christmas. Bertha has cried a good deal in the kitchen, but I have been too much of a coward to ask why. I've even pretended not to notice. But of course I've known all along that it had to come out."

William grunted as he lit his pipe. Talk about servants was always distasteful. One paid for peace in the home.

"What's wrong with Susan?" he demanded. He had put this off, too, until the meal was over, but now they might as well face everything at once.

"It's Pete," Elinor said. "He has never forgiven her for letting Jessica have the dog. They are quarreling all the time, and it takes her mind from her work. I don't like the way she looks. She is actually getting thin."

"I wish she'd forget the fellow."

"I think she does, too, but she can't. There's something—"

Herbert came in with the coffee and she broke off. He set the cups carefully before her on a small table, his big hands trembling slightly, as even William could see.

"Very well, Herbert," Elinor said.

The man stood then between them and stepped back somewhat so that they saw his face, that fat flabby absurd face, the pinched nose, the small lipless mouth, the lashless little grey eyes, the stiff black hair which no brush or lotion would smooth down. A common fellow, William thought, a shape of ordinary clay, hiding what low passions—

67

Then came the horror. Herbert did not speak. Instead he began silently to cry and this with only the slightest disarrangement of his pudgy features. The tight mouth twitched, out of the little eyes tears rolled down the pasty cheeks and fell upon the white starched house coat in grey and viscid spots.

"Oh, Herbert, please don't," Elinor murmured.

Herbert sniffed and felt for his handkerchief and not finding it, he wiped his nose with the back of his hand. William looked away, resisting the thought that he ought to offer Herbert his own clean handkerchief. He could not do it. Instead he gazed into the fire while Herbert went on sniffing until he was able to speak, sobbing short gasps.

"I give her—everything, Mrs. Asher!"

"I'm sure you do," Elinor said, comforting while William sat motionless gazing into the fire.

"Two vacuum cleaners, one upstairs, Mrs. Asher, on account of she ain't strong and it was heavy liftin' the machine here up and down—"

"Very kind of you," Elinor said crisply.

"She don't like the livin' room rug, she wants an all over like this one here—two hundred dollars, Mrs. Asher, ma'am."

"I hope she will appreciate it," Elinor said.

The sniffling began again. William glanced swiftly and saw the massive face trembling in a jelly of pain.

"She won't let me come near her—"

Ah, here it was—the eternal accusation between man and wife!

"Night after night—my health's gettin' ruined—"

Elinor took hold resolutely. "It's very strange. Does she give a reason?"

"No reason, Mrs. Asher. Just says she—can't."

"I simply don't know how to advise you, Herbert," Elinor said.

"No, ma'am, nor you, sir, I don't expect it. I used to handle it myself before. She hasn't no real stren'th."

"Before what?" William asked, suddenly turning his head.

"Before she got the dog," Herbert sobbed. "It's that beast, sir, it lays between us on the floor—she would have them twin beds before she'd marry me. He lays there, ready to jump at me—she just calls him—"

"What a dreadful thing!" Elinor whispered.

Herbert stood, his heavy head drooping, sniffling unevenly, trembling from head to foot.

"Why don't you get rid of the dog?" William demanded. Here was a hideous thing to go through with after dinner in his own house! His quick imagination, the bane of his soul, uncontrollable, created the bedroom scene, the lustful man, the terrified woman, that red-eyed beast between, its scruff standing.

"She says if I do, she'll—leave me." Herbert's voice rose into a squeak of final agony.

"That's ridiculous," Elinor said in a voice of hearty common sense. "She'll probably respect you for it."

"I daren't—take the chance. She's queer in some ways you wouldn't expect."

Elinor sat up in her chair. "Herbert, stop crying, please. We can't discuss this sensibly while you stand there looking like that. If you cry before Jessica, it will really make her despise you. No woman could bear it."

She spoke cruelly, her voice hard and clear, but it was a relief to hear it like a knife of steel, cutting through the mush of the clogged atmosphere of Herbert.

It did no good to Herbert, however. "Hankishiff," he muttered in a strangled voice and rushed from the room.

Neither of them spoke for minutes. Then Elinor poured the coffee. "Sugar?" she asked.

Sometimes William wanted sugar, sometimes he did not.

"Clear and black," he said and took the cup.

She had broken the brunt of it and he should say something.

"A horrible revelation," he said drily. "Revolting, repulsive, it should never have been made. We can do nothing about it."

Elinor did not answer at once. Then she said, "I do feel sorry for Jessica."

He was surprised, for he had thought until now that she had some impatience with Jessica, an unrecognized jealousy he might have said, strictly to himself, because Jessica was pretty and because she had seen this young and pretty woman put her hands on Edwin's shoulders, appealing, in Jessica's own way, to every man, something which Elinor herself had never done and could never have done simply because of her own straightforward soul, and not because she did not know, as of course she did, that her own high beauty was far beyond anything, even now, that Jessica possessed.

"Still, you know," he remonstrated.

"There's no 'still' about it," Elinor broke in sharply. "I know exactly what you are going to say and I am surprised at you, William, for you so seldom say what any man would say."

"What was I about to say?" he inquired with purposeful mildness.

"You were going to say that after all Herbert is her husband, that it is right and natural that he should expect to have sexual intercourse, and what does a man marry for?"

He was too honest to manufacture anything else. It was true that he had been about to say this, although certainly not in such bold words.

"You put it very crudely," he said with dignity.

"I put it as it is," Elinor said. "It is a crude business."

"But the dog—" he protested.

"I'm glad Jessica has the dog," Elinor said almost rudely.

He was amazed at her. He put down his coffee cup and gazed at her. This aspect he had never seen and he did not like it. Where might a man find security if not with his wife after twenty-five years of marriage? A woman ought not to reveal new aspects after that. It was unfair, disturbing, upsetting the very citadel of the home.

"My dear," he said, "you sound bitter."

"I feel bitter," Elinor said vigorously. She poured herself a cup of coffee, and it occurred to him that all this time she had not lifted her head to look at him.

"Why?" he demanded looking at her bent head.

"That Herbert," she exclaimed, "so soft, so fat, so demanding! I know exactly how Jessica feels. Every woman does."

This was frightening. She made it personal, she dragged it here between them, something obscene, the sort of thing a decent man never faces, certainly not in himself.

"Let's not discuss it," he said.

They sat in silence then, drinking their coffee.

All this distracted William's mind from Susan, and it was only when Elinor spoke of their child again a week later at Atlantic City that he remembered there was also Peter Dobbs. They were sitting in a warm corner of the sandy beach, sheltered from an inconsiderate west wind by the boardwalk. It was too cold to think of going into the water, which nevertheless looked temptingly clear and mild, the surf small and guileless. He was not a strong swimmer and he did not like the crushing surf of summertime; it was one of the lesser cruelties of nature, he

71

thought, that in the winter when the water was too cold for the human frame the sea was often smooth, the waves subdued at least when the sky was cloudless as today it was, whereas in summer some tempestuous aspect of the moon compelled the tides to restlessness. Eve, made from the rib of Adam, was only the legend of the perverse and female moon torn from the side of the newly created globe of billions of years ago, and the gaping wound of the Pacific basin, raw basalt at the bottom, was still as unhealed as man himself. And here was the moon as he had seen it last night, whirling above the yearning earth, remote and unreachable, never again to be joined, and yet pulling the earth's tides toward herself, only to reject them again and again in the ceaseless rise and fall of the rhythms of untiring creation.

Lying on his back, his eyes closed to the sun, he felt those rhythms in his own being and he reached for Elinor's hand. She gave it willingly and he pressed it against his cheek, a miracle today as it had been years ago; not the same, for the hand had changed, grown harder, perhaps, certainly more firm, but still his Elinor's hand.

"Susan wants to come down," Elinor said.

"Did she telephone?" he asked.

"Yes, this morning while you were still asleep. She wants to come down tomorrow. She says she has to talk to us."

He sighed and pressing her hand he let it fall to the sand. "Then I suppose she must."

"I think so."

It was extraordinary how children could continue to intrude. One expected it when they were babies, and Susan would have been the first to insist upon her womanhood, did he call her still his child. Nevertheless for him the carefree morning was over, though it was two hours

72

until they could go into the hotel for lunch. He could not feel alone with Elinor any more until Susan had come and gone, had made known her new problem, whatever it was, for the lives of the young were, it seemed, thorny with inexplicable and insoluble problems. The entire web of his law practice, fraught with the crimes underlying the life of the greatest city in the world, was not as agitating as the militant demand of the problems of his three grown children, Winsten, the young father, Edwin, the lover, and Susan, the eternal female. Or perhaps it was only that he could get up from his desk, close the door of his city office and walk away, whereas these three who were his children, inescapably his own being, continued in him and were forever in his home, their childish ghosts persistent in his very blood. He could no more escape them than he could escape himself.

Nevertheless, he was not prepared even by a day and a night of wondering what was the matter now with Susan. She appeared the next morning, nearer noon than dawn, whirling up to the hotel entrance as he could see from the window where he had gone to examine his second best tie, a dark blue and gray stripe of which he was fond but which he suspected of becoming threadbare. He was not a vain man but Susan was critical of him as a possession. There in the hotel driveway he saw her small dark red convertible, which she had teased out of him as an early graduation present, and to his unutterable horror he saw Peter Dobbs leaping over the door, one long leg after the other, then opening the door for Susan.

"Elinor!" So he shouted through the connecting bathroom. "She's brought that fellow from the Ozarks with her!"

"Oh no!" Elinor cried back, but she came, looking quite pretty in her pink silk slip, and he wondered why it

was that the face of a slender woman must fade first.
Elinor in her pink slip was otherwise still a young girl.

She stood behind the curtain, drawing it across her as a
screen, and he saw the nape of her neck, the little silvery
curls there, threaded with blonde hairs. He remembered
that when they were first married the little pale gold curls
on the nape of her neck were irresistible, and he bent
forward suddenly and kissed them again now.

She turned to smile at him brightly. "Now, William,
we must get dressed quickly. She'll be running up here—"

"Of course!" he grumbled. He considered explaining to
her that the kiss he had given her was not the beginning
of something at this moment, but a souvenir from their
bridal morning. Another time he might have explained,
but the fear of Susan bringing that great black-haired
fellow upstairs made explanation impossible. Besides,
Elinor should have known. But she still suspected him, as
he supposed all women suspected all men, of the poten-
tial and instantaneous passion which he had not known
how to manage in the early days, but which now, alas, or
perhaps luckily, he was quite used to curbing, subduing
or allowing, according to the faint hints she permitted to
escape her. There was nothing actually stereotyped about
their love. She could and did often surprise him. But it
was a cat and mouse business, and sometimes he felt
that more often than he knew he was the mouse.

Susan was by now actually at the door, but Elinor was
dressed and looking composed, although the top button of
her blouse was unbuttoned as usual, and he felt sensitive
about that black beast of the mountains observing such
a detail. To Susan it would not have mattered, but he
preserved the jealousy of his generation and yet still he
could not mention it to Elinor, although she was so calm
he guessed that she knew what he was feeling and would
have none of it.

There was no time, however. The door burst open and they stood there, the young and healthy creatures, gay with their news which was obvious to anyone looking at them. They were in love, some sort of love at least, and William felt his scalp prickle. Elinor was looking at them strangely, her blue eyes intense.

"Mother and Dad!" Susan cried dramatically, "Pete and I are engaged. We thought we'd better tell you."

"Come in," William said. "I should think you had. When did it happen?"

Susan shrieked laughter. "Oh, Dad, as though it just happened!"

They came in, and he noticed that Elinor said nothing. She sat down on one of the two stuffed chairs, and the two young creatures sat on the narrow sofa. Entirely shameless, Pete wrapped his long right arm about Susan, and she caught his right hand under her left arm and held it pressed to her waist.

"It's such a relief to have it over," she cried in the same excited voice. "I didn't really know my own mind until he asked me, at last, day before yesterday. I did and I didn't. When I thought he never was going to ask me, I thought I didn't. The rest of the time I did."

William listened to this and for the first time since he saw his daughter born, red with her recent efforts and rebellious apparently even against birth, he found her repulsive. The nakedness of the triumphant female nowadays was nothing less than repulsive. What hidden aspect of Elinor had taken this modern shape in their daughter? Elinor at least was modest.

"Why don't one of you say something?" Susan demanded.

William refused to answer this but Elinor was heroic. "How nice," she murmured through pallid lips.

Susan and Pete burst into a duet of loud laughter. "Oh,

Mother," Susan sighed, drunk with laughter. "Isn't she priceless, Pete? Isn't she wonderful? Nice! Didn't I tell you?"

"Yeah," Pete grunted. His black eyes were glittering bright; for the first time William saw him awake.

He felt an immense anger. "I wonder if you two have any imagination," he said sharply. "I wonder if, short of waiting a quarter of a century, you can imagine how it feels when a child who has absorbed time and funds—not to mention love—suddenly turns up with a perfect stranger to whom she announces herself engaged. Does it occur to you," he went on magisterially, gazing at his daughter, "whether we might perhaps ask, as a return for benefits received, that we be given some opportunity of acquaintance with the stranger before we are compelled to accept him as our son-in-law?"

The sound of his voice was impressive, even in his own ears. He had never heard it more so when he pleaded his cases before obdurate judges.

Susan looked puzzled. She opened her dark eyes wide, a trick he remembered from her childhood, when, compelled in due course to reprove her, she had looked up at him with these same large eyes. She leaned forward in the circle of Pete's arm.

"Are you serious, Dad?" So she inquired, wondering, as he could see, quite genuinely.

He was about to protest his seriousness when Elinor broke in.

"Of course he's not serious. It's a shock and he doesn't know what to say. It's none of our business. If you choose Pete, it's welcome to you, Pete."

She smiled her warmest and most charming smile and William stared at her, stirred by her reasonless desertion. Had he not been protecting her? What did it matter to him whom the children chose? He was used now to doing without them. This Susan was not the small dark exquisite child, so plump and fragrant, who used to curl into his arms before she went to bed. She had left his house, in spirit, long ago. Her heart was not there. He had read of countries where the daughter was never considered a permanent member of the family because when she married she belonged by the heart to a strange man's family. Therefore why educate her and why spend upon her the treasures of parental love? He recognized this sympathy with dim guilt as a subterranean jealousy which disgusted him. At what age, he inquired of himself, did the beast in a man finally surrender unconditionally?

"What are you thinking about, Dad?" Susan asked curiously.

"Nothing that you would understand," he retorted. He gathered himself together with effort.

"Has he an income?" he inquired, not looking at Pete.

"Gas station," Pete said amiably.

"He owns it," Susan said proudly.

It was the second blow. A gas station? For this he had tenderly nurtured his daughter, had even paid for lessons on the violin, enduring without articulate complaint the primary years of wailing discord, until she was at last very good indeed. "I suppose you know," her music master had said to him only a few months ago, "your daughter can do about as she likes with music. She is very near the professional level."

With frightful control he put the next question gently. "Where is this gas station?"

"Highway near my home," Pete said. "Lots of tourists to the Ozarks nowadays."

Elinor spoke with pale lips. "Shall you like to go so far away, Susan?"

"Yes," Susan said robustly. "I shall love it."

There was nothing much to be said after that. Elinor,

77

who had envied the parents of Winsten's wife the long
pleasure of a carefully arranged wedding for a bride,
was silenced. She was probably thinking, as he was,
William imagined. What was the use of a beautiful and
expensive wedding, when the next step was to a gas
station?

"Oughtn't we to have lunch?" Elinor asked. She glanced
at the small circle of diamonds on her wrist that held
the watch he had given her upon their twenty-fifth wedding anniversary. "The dining room will be crowded if
we wait."

"We're starved," Susan agreed. "At least I am, and
Pete is always hungry."

"Always kin eat," Pete agreed, unfolding himself from
the sofa.

So they went downstairs, and William was glad not
to be alone with the strangers. Susan was a stranger,
too, he had lost her finally this morning, and all that
he had left was the ghost of the child she had been,
that and nothing more. He sat down at a small round
table at which they were all crowded, and examined
the menu carefully. Rejecting the array of seafood and
steaks he chose baked beans and brown bread and ate
them, after a long wait, in complete silence, listening
not to the chattering rise and fall of the voices around
him but to the rising thunder of the surf outside. The
tide was coming in.

The moment William reached home on Friday, as
though he had not been disturbed enough by Susan,
Herbert waylaid him in the hall.

"I'd like a word or two with you, sir, if it's convenient."

It was not convenient. William was tired, the week
in his office had been peculiarly exhausting after his
absence, and he had wondered on the way home whether
he were getting too old for the grind. All those hours

Herbert had sat in the chauffeur's seat, speechless. Now liberated by his white house coat he wanted time from his employer. Time, William felt rebelliously, was the one treasure he had left. Money was of little worth, half of his wage went to supporting a government he could not approve, and his children had left him. Time, and especially time with Elinor, was what he could not spare. But the demand of one's inferiors could not be refused, as he would have refused curtly enough any man who was his equal. He hired secretaries for nothing else than to protect him from requests for his time, but at home he was defenseless.

"Very well, Herbert," he said with grim patience. "We had better go into the library at once. We have fifteen or twenty minutes before dinner."

Herbert followed with noiseless and solemn tread and when William had sat down he closed the door and stood against it. There he began soundlessly to weep as he had before, his big flat face quivering and trembling and his tight lips twitching. This could only mean Jessica again!

"Come—come," William said, repelled anew and trying not to be impatient.

Herbert sniffed stealthily, searched for his handkerchief with the same stealthy air, found it and wiped his face.

"You know the black dog, sir?"

"Yes, I remember the beast," William replied.

"Well, that dog, sir, it seems she's got to care for it more than any earthly creetur, more than her mother or even me, her lawful husband."

"Sit down," William said.

Herbert turned and locked the door. Then he tiptoed three steps forward and sat down on the edge of one

79

of the straight oaken chairs. His flabby jowls trembled again and William looked away.

"That black dog," Herbert said, clearing his throat, "bit a little kid last week. It was a farmer's kid next to our farm. She come over to git some eggs. They take eggs off us onct a week. She's about seven or eight years old. The dog bit her in the thigh. It wasn't the first time, either. He bit her onct before on the hand."

"I trust the dog isn't mad," William said gravely.

Herbert did not heed the interruption. He went on, his voice dreadful and whispering. "I told her—Jessica, that is—that we ought not to keep a dog that bites kids. When we have a kid of our own—did I tell you she was expecting?"

"No," William said.

"Yes," Herbert said, "she's due in June. I told her we ought to get rid of that dog when it bit the kid the first time. She wouldn't hear to it and I let it go. She was pregnant and I thought it was a notion. Now the dog has bit the kid again, and the kid's father says he'll sue me. It's a real deep bite. The kid is in the hospital to get it cauterized. Can I be sued?"

"It depends," William said cautiously.

"On what?"

"Let me consider it for a few days," William said.

"The kid's father is liable to sue me for a thousand dollars maybe," Herbert said.

"I'll let you know," William said. It was absurd that he should take his priceless time for a dog bite. He felt his anger rise against Pete, who had brought the savage beast to his house and now he could not be rid of it.

Herbert wadded the handkerchief into a ball and dabbed at one eye and the other. "You probably think it's queer I cry, sir." His voice slid into a hysterical squeak.

"It's not just the dog now. It's her. I don't know what to make of Jessica, sir."

"What's the matter now with Jessica?" William asked, not wanting to know. He glanced at the locked door. A moment more and he would get up and unlock it.

"She's turning on her mother to hate her, like," Herbert said, his voice falling to a whisper. "We can't make it out. Her mother considers her like the apple of her eye, you might say, if you understand that saying, sir. The old lady spends her spare time with us, naturally, and we have fixed up a room for her upstairs, a nice corner room, which is only right, since the house is hers until after she dies, it's in her will to come to Jessica and me, of course, after that, but I had expected to have the old lady with us when she gets too old for the job here which I figure might be any time, and then I figured maybe Jessica and I could work here and the old lady could take care of the kids we might have by then. I don't want a lot of kids, two is plenty, and then I thought I'd let Jessica get herself tied, which she wanted to do in the very beginning."

"Tied?" William inquired.

"Her toobes," Herbert explained, "so she won't get pregnant. You can get a doctor to do it, if she's nervous. She is nervous and that's the truth. The doctor says so himself."

"Indeed," William said, once more deeply revolted.

"I wouldn't hear to its being done right away," Herbert went on. Voice and face were solemn and the tears drying on his cheeks had left the glistening wake of snails.

"No—no," William said unhappily. "I feel sorry for Bertha," he added. "Someone should talk with Jessica. Perhaps Mrs. Asher will do so."

"Would she?" Herbert asked eagerly. "That's what I

wanted to know could I ask. It would bring Jessica to her senses, like. She's that fond of Mrs. Asher's family."

"Very well," William said. He got up determined to unlock the door, but Herbert hastened toward it first. He turned the key and stood impressively holding the door wide, while William passed through, bestowing a slight nod of acknowledgment.

Upstairs he found Elinor putting dried lavender from last year's garden between the garments in her bureau drawers.

They kissed, and he sniffed the clean fragrance. How many women, he wondered, put lavender between their garments nowadays instead of some French sachet? He disliked all French perfumes, though once he had thought them enchanting. Vermont had made the change. French perfumes were foreign here.

"Has Bertha complained to you of Jessica's behavior?" he asked.

"She has been grumpy," Elinor said, "but she has not mentioned Jessica."

"Herbert tells me Jessica has turned completely against Bertha. He took me into the library and locked the door and confided to me a mixture of complaints. I won't go into them all, but somehow I promised that you would speak to Jessica."

"Oh dear," Elinor said.

"I'm very sorry," William said. "I don't know how it happened. I wanted to get rid of him, I suppose."

"Well, I'd better hear Jessica's side of it first," Elinor said sighing. "Bertha gets so upset and then she goes to bed. I can't have her going to bed this weekend. Edwin is coming home tomorrow."

"What for?" Were they never to be alone?

"Have you forgotten it is his spring vacation?"

He had forgotten. Now that Winsten was fairly stabilized in Boston in his own small house with wife and children, now that Susan had gone blithely to the Ozarks to visit Pete's family, for that was where she was, an unthinkable liberty, but she had laughed when he suggested some sort of a chaperone, he had supposed that he and Elinor could live in some peace for the next few weeks. He had even thought of persuading her to go to New York with him for some of the last theater of the season.

"I think Vera will decide this week whether she'll marry Edwin," Elinor was saying.

"It is high time," William said. He wanted to get them all settled, all his children.

"Wouldn't it be nice," Elinor now said, "if we had robots in the house instead of servants?"

He sank down upon a chair. "Robots? They'd develop some devilish temperament of their own. What is Herbert or Jessica but a handful of chemicals mixed with a lot of water? It's the proportion. When everything is all in some damned relationship to everything else, something new emerges, a creature, a personality. It's fission. Even the atom won't explode until the combination is just right—"

Elinor stood listening, her arms hanging at her sides. "You're low, aren't you?"

"Peace," William said. "It's all I want."

A fine strange thing, he thought, the way human beings destroyed their own peace while most earnestly desiring peace above all else, and destroyed it in secret subterranean ways, obstinately maintaining their own wilfulness, as Jessica was doing, the upheaval in that small farm dwelling he had never seen reaching even into his own stately house. And why had he and Elinor not the courage to repudiate these creatures who disturbed them so causelessly? He watched Elinor as she moved about the room and understood her as he understood himself, that neither of them had the courage to be ruthless. They could not, out of something that was not weakness, he believed, cut off a human being who was helpless within their periphery, as surely Jessica was. Jessica was a child, innocent and gentle, between the two monoliths of Bertha and Herbert. She must be rescued, she could be rescued.

"Cousin Emma said that she wished she had taken Jessica to New York with her, before that marriage," he said suddenly.

Elinor sat down to ponder. "It might have been a good thing, but it is too late. Jessica is married."

"I have a feeling that we ought to get together today and see exactly what her circumstances are," he said. "I'd like to have the matter settled in my mind. It is very difficult to deal with Herbert when he stands and blubbers."

"He's disgusting," Elinor said vehemently. "A man in tears turns my stomach."

William found himself moved to defense. "I suppose there are times when a man must weep also."

"Weeping should be done in secret," Elinor said.

It occurred to him again that indeed he had rarely seen her weep and not for years. He asked with intense diffidence and after a long moment, "Do you weep in secret, my dearest?"

She was evasive as always when he approached the depths between them, which was the Vermont in her, he supposed, or perhaps only the Winsten, so long in Vermont. "I learned long ago not to weep about anything," she said.

"Did you once?" he pressed.

"Perhaps," she said almost with indifference, "when I was younger, before I understood life."

He went no further, a natural fear or shyness preventing him, or perhaps only the reluctance of the aging to turn up one's own past, as buried, as irretrievable, as the centuries before one's birth.

He got up with energy enough to dismiss it all, saying, "At any rate, let us go and see Jessica."

"Shall I tell Bertha?" Elinor asked.

They looked at each other uncertainly and he laughed. "We are absurd, the matter is of no importance, the quarrels of servants, and we feel as though we were discussing the affairs of nations. Tell her by all means and what if she does go to bed? We'll do for ourselves."

His hardihood decided her. "You must come with me, for she is afraid of you at least and she thinks nothing of me, because she saw me the day I was born."

They went together down the stairs and into Bertha's kitchen where she stood before the stove, her thick legs planted wide, upholding the mountain of her body. She did not turn her head when they came in, and their courage dwindled. But William felt Elinor quail first, and he summoned his remote sense of humor. What, must two educated resourceful cultivated persons be cowed by the mass simplicity of a Bertha?

"Bertha," he said decisively, "Mrs. Asher and I have been talking about Jessica. We would like to go and visit her today and see why she seems so unhappy with Herbert."

Bertha began to weep, not turning her head and continuing to stir gravy in a skillet. Her huge frame quivered, haunches, shoulders, the massive neck. "I losted my home," she moaned. She dabbed her eyes with her huge red hand. "She's turned against me, mine own childt! She don't vant I shouldt come home even for Sunday, no, and

85

she says she don't vant I shouldt come home on birt-dayss, and not on Christmas yet. She tellt Herbert I beated her hard venn she vass liddle."

She turned slowly, her big face a wreckage of sorrow, she demanded of Elinor, "Didt I effer beat her, Miss Elinor, you tell me, only venn she vendt into your haus, the parlors, and like she vass one of you? Ya, I see her, and so I muss beat her. It iss not her haus, I tellt her, you shtay in kitchen vere we belongs, not im haus. Only so I beat her, because she dondt lissen. She goes und she goes, sitting on welwet chairs, playing pianos, looking in mirrors, so I beat her."

William listening, caught the gleam of a thread of reason, a quick illumination. This then was the explanation of Jessica posing before the mirrors. Even as a child she had begun to live the dream of herself in the big house, not belonging to the kitchen and therefore not, oh never, to Bertha, the cook, and scarcely to Heinrich the butler. She was somebody else, a lovely girl, somebody perhaps even belonging to the family who really lived in the big house, who owned it, certainly as she could not except through dreams. His sensitive mind, his swift imagination, the qualities which underlay his work as a lawyer and made him understand why crimes were committed enlightened him now, and he was warm with pity for the little child beaten for her dreams, incurable dreams which she still wove. He was glad that he had not told Elinor about the scenes before the mirror.

Bertha was talking through thick sobs. "Can I let her get out of kitchens and maybe Misses Winsten fire me and Heinrich? Only so I beat her, maybe *ein, drei, vier* times, not effery day like she tells it now. She tells it to Herbert and he lofs her so silly he beliefs it. He don't want me in mine own *haus*, nieder."

"Herbert?" Elinor repeated, mystified.

"Ya, him," Bertha said, and seizing her large apron she wept into it, the gravy spoon uplifted like a signal above her bent head.

"We will go and see for ourselves," William said sternly.

"Don't cry, Bertha," Elinor said. She patted the heavy shoulder. "Oh, please don't cry! You'll always have a home here, Bertha."

William looked at Elinor, aghast. She had committed them! She had promised an eternal home to Bertha, the aging, pig-headed, tenderhearted, bad-tempered old woman who was slave and tyrant together. Aghast they stole from the kitchen, and faced each other in the living room.

"Still, we can't turn Bertha out in the streets, William," Elinor said.

"No," he agreed. That was the trouble with life. The old and the poor, the ignorant, the helpless, the young, even a beast, could not just be turned out into the streets when they became nuisances. They had to be sheltered, though under one's own roof.

They were diverted at this moment, if not cheered, by the early arrival of Edwin, neat and debonair in his usual fashion. It occurred to William to recognize now the value in this second son, the calmness of his young face, the competence of his manner, the composure unusual for one so young.

"Let us take Edwin and Vera with us when we go to see Jessica," he suggested, turning to Elinor.

He explained briefly, and Edwin nodded. "It sounds queer, I'd like to go. I've always been fond of Jessica, in a way. She's never seemed quite like a servant. If she wants to leave Herbert, she might come to Vera and me when we're married."

87

Elinor clasped her hands in joy. "Has Vera decided? Oh, Edwin!"

He nodded. "She really has. She decided last night. She said she wanted it settled before she came today."

"Oh, darling," Elinor said fondly. She seldom kissed her grown children but now she went to this reliable son and kissed his cheek. "I am so happy. I dearly love Vera."

He blushed, his blue eyes shone, he embraced her warmly. "She adores you both," he said, his calm young voice cracking a little. "I am really bringing you another daughter."

The affair of Jessica disappeared in the mists of their immediate content and they allowed him to leave again almost immediately that he might fetch Vera.

"Now we must wait until tomorrow to see Jessica," Elinor said happily. "I wonder where Edwin's wedding will be? I suppose they'll want it in Manchester, in the Episcopal church."

"Just so Vera's father doesn't want it in his bank," William said with returning humor. A happy marriage was a good omen for the whole family, a young and happy marriage, as his and Elinor's had been and had continued to be, even when youth was gone. Unusual sentiment warmed his heart and he felt moved to turn and take his wife in his arms and kiss her full on the mouth.

"Why, William," she cried.

"I suddenly remember myself when young," he explained.

She wavered for only a moment and then she yielded gracefully to his arms and returned his kiss, without ardor but with full consent.

Thus the next morning after an evening made delightful by the tactful tenderness of Edwin, who somehow made his parents believe that he was in no haste for them to retire early, they rose from the breakfast table and prepared to visit Jessica. Vera liked the early morning, she never lay abed after the fashion of Susan, and she had already taken an early walk with Edwin before breakfast. Fresh as a single-petaled rose, her straight blonde hair bright and smooth, her fair skin delicately pink upon her cheeks, she presented as nearly a perfect picture of the desirable daughter-in-law as William could imagine. He could imagine, too, exactly the sort of wife she would make for Edwin, a loyal, faithful, steadfast woman, pretty enough to be pleasant and not so pretty as to be dangerous under any circumstances.

Her well-cut blue suit was smart enough, expensive of course, but worth the money and it would wear well. Everything about Vera would wear well. There was nothing sportive in her. Though she had given her promise to Edwin only day before yesterday, a scant thirty-six hours ago, yet already there was about her the air of the faithful wife. He was glad that Edwin deserved her. Vera was too pure a gold to be given into hands less honorable than Edwin's. It was all very suitable, and this was perhaps praise enough.

They set forth in the old grey car, the country car they called it, Edwin driving, and after half an hour or so, they left the macadam and turned down a rutted dirt road, which led them some miles across a low mountain into a spreading valley. Herbert and Bertha had seen them off, Bertha on the verge of recurring tears, and Herbert giving solemn directions regarding Clayton Corners where anybody except himself would take the wrong turn, five roads meeting together as they did, the center of a star.

"You take the worst road, sir. I been aimin' to get that road fixed but the township is short of funds—always is."

The worst road was entirely obvious and they chose it

unerringly for another five miles to draw up before the house which they recognized from Herbert's description.

"We must be careful of that miserable cur," William exclaimed, peering from the window.

The dog, however, was chained. They saw it at once. The immense black frame crawled out of the large kennel, it rushed the length of the thick iron chain, roaring at them, bellowing until the hills echoed.

Almost immediately Jessica opened the front door and came out to meet them. She was beautifully dressed, pregnant as they could see, but the soft wool stuff of her suit, a full skirt, a smart little jacket falling over her waist, concealed the harshness of her shape. Her face was thin, her blue eyes were ethereal and ethereal was her smile as she held out her hands to them.

"Oh, how welcome you are," she cried in her pretty voice. "I feel as though you were my own family, coming to see me at last!"

She came forward. Elinor kissed her upon a sudden impulse and William found himself holding both her hands. Vera and Edwin stood to one side, waiting, and Jessica turned to them.

"Mr. Edwin," she said uncertainly.

"You remember Vera," Edwin began.

"Oh, I do," Jessica interrupted him. "I do indeed remember! It is good of you to come."

"We are to be married," Edwin said somewhat abruptly.

Jessica looked bewildered for a moment, almost hurt.

"Married? Are you—" she hesitated and laughed softly. "Of course you are. I forgot you are a man. I always think of you as a boy."

Jessica's sweet blue eyes lingered wistfully upon Vera's quiet face. "And how old are you?"

"I am a year younger than Edwin," Vera said quietly.

"Oh, that is so wise," Jessica cried softly. "It is always wise to be younger—not too much, but just a year or so. Come in, come in—"

They did not know what to make of her manner, she threw a light contrived fascination over all she said and did, her narrow hands moved here and there, now at her throat, now at her hair, and she smiled incessantly, a bright and brittle glitter about her face, her great blue eyes shining. She was like a foreigner, come from a country they did not know, whose customs were not theirs, whose thoughts they could not fathom even through the common language.

"Come in—come in," she repeated in a sort of floating ecstasy, and she led the way into the house, a farmhouse, but strangely unlike what William had imagined. The front door gave into a narrow hall from which a straight flight of steps led up to the second floor. The conventional rooms, parlor to the left, dining room to the right, opened from the hall. They entered the parlor, and William looked about him, seeing vaguely familiar settings. Suddenly he understood the strangeness of the room. In her way this astounding creature Jessica had tried to imitate his own home! Between the windows opposite the door hung the mirror, the two wall candlesticks, underneath which was a really good imitation of his walnut escritoire, at either end of the room were the tall book cabinets, not so large, of course, as his and certainly not antiques. Upon the mantelpiece were china figures, though not Dresden. His eyes met Elinor's and they exchanged amazement and pity.

"What a pretty room," Vera said.

"I don't like the carpet," Jessica said eagerly. "It's a cheap thing. The one I want costs two hundred dollars. Herbert says we can't afford it." She laughed, her eyes suddenly diamond-hard. "But I'll get it! I don't worry any

91

more about such things. Would you like to go upstairs and see all the rooms? The house is much too small, of course, but we are planning to build, and then this house will just be used for the servants. I have the place chosen, up on the hill."

She parted the net curtains hanging between the blue velveteen draperies.

"I want to see you, not the house," Elinor said with sudden firmness. "Sit down, Jessica."

"Vera and I will walk about outside," Edwin said. They had not sat down.

"Oh no, indeed," Jessica cried in her highest most silvery tones. "You must sit down, Edwin. There is nothing hidden from you. I have never had secrets from you, have I? Never!"

Edwin, astonished, sat down. They all sat down, bemused by unreality.

"When do you expect the baby?" Elinor asked quietly.

"Oh, I don't know," Jessica said. Her strangely innocent face turned upon them radiantly. "I don't think about it, Mrs. Asher. It seems so useless, just having children. Children have children have children have children—isn't it all just useless? Over and over and over and over! And what is there here for children? No streets to walk upon, no shop windows, no movies, no drugstores, nothing to amuse them. So I just don't think about it."

Elinor interrupted this. "Your mother tells me you have quarrels with her."

Jessica flung up her hands. They were very white and thin, the nails painted a shell pink. Who, William wondered, washed the dishes and scrubbed the floors? Herbert perhaps, fatuous as he was, or Bertha, on the rare days when she came home. Only now she was not to be allowed to come.

"Indeed I don't quarrel with Mamma," Jessica declared.

"I have simply said I will never see her any more, as long as I live, that's all."

"You are living in her house," William said abruptly.

"Only until we build upon the hill," she said brightly. "Then this house will just be used for the servants."

"Your mother?" he asked grimly.

"Oh no," Jessica said. "I will never see her again." She leaned forward, her cheeks suddenly scarlet. "I don't suppose you ever knew, Mr. Asher, but my mother used to beat me terribly. She is a very cruel woman."

"Jessica, I don't believe you," Elinor said. "In all the years that Bertha has been in our house I have never heard anybody else say that."

"That's because you are the family," Jessica said and then the words burst from the pent spring within her, her eyes widened, the lids snapping, as she looked from one face to the other. She rushed on, the clearly articulated words like a ripple of falling crystals. "She used to beat me and hold her great fist over my mouth so I couldn't cry! She beat me until I felt as though my very bones were split and my poor father was helpless. He would stand there wringing his hands, he would get down on his knees, speechless, because he didn't want the family to hear, and just on the other side of the pantry door, you were all sitting in riches and safety, while I was being beaten, and all in such quiet—"

The terrible drama was displayed before them in the frightful intensity of Jessica's being. She flamed, she quivered, her eyes were wild and immense, her voice as edged as the high string of a violin.

"I cannot believe it," Elinor insisted.

"Oh, you never could believe," Jessica cried. "None of you have ever believed me, only Edwin—Edwin, my darling!"

She turned and gazed at Edwin, melting, her whole

frame relaxing, softening, yearning. "You knew, didn't you, Edwin? I told you everything."

Edwin stared. "I don't know what you are talking about," he said in a clear voice.

"Oh yes, you do, my darling," Jessica said, coaxing him. The white hands fluttered toward him, they clasped each other. "Don't be afraid, you will have to tell your bride, and now I can tell Herbert. I have kept it all a beautiful secret until now. But Herbert will have to know at last."

"Jessica!" William said sternly, seeing his son's face.

She paid no heed to him, the words flowed on, softly, freely, swept upon her apparent love. "Don't you remember, Edwin? Can you forget? Don't you remember the long lovely day we spent together in the hotel in New York? I met you there, do you remember? The one day, my one perfect day in all my life! Ah, don't be afraid to remember!"

Edwin leaped to his feet. He turned to Vera, his face white, even his lips dry and white. "Vera, I assure you, I don't know what she is talking about."

Vera rose, too. "I know you do not." She put her hand in his arm. "Let's go outside and wait." But she was suddenly very pale.

They went out and Elinor watched them, and William appalled and dazed, glanced at her, and then stared at Jessica. Jessica was smiling gently, her eyes upon the floor, seeing nothing.

"Poor Edwin," she said softly, "he has not the courage to say he remembers. But I shall never forget—never! It was I who refused him at last, Mrs. Asher. I knew that the family would never accept me. And how could I live in the house, with my mother in the kitchen? Of course I could have dismissed her. That could have been done. But I refused my love. Now I know how wrong that was. Love must never be refused, lead where it may.

I have lost everything, except that one lovely day—with him. And I shall never see my mother again."

"Jessica, you are lying," William said. "You know that there never was such a day." He made his voice loud, to penetrate the charm.

"Oh yes, indeed there was, and indeed and indeed," Jessica said softly, positively. She laid her clasped hands upon her bosom. "It is here forever."

"William, let's go home," Elinor said. She rose and did not put out her hand. "Jessica, I, too, do not believe one word of what you say. But you must never again tell such lies. I shall tell Herbert myself that I think you are either very ill or very wicked. I feel sorry for both Herbert and your mother."

She walked from the room and William followed. He turned his head once to look back. Jessica sat with her hands clasped on her bosom, smiling, as though she did not see them go. There was something very wrong.

Outside, the four of them climbed into the car and drove away in silence. For what was there to say? What was Vera thinking and what lay in the mind of Edwin, his son, and did Elinor doubt her son, in spite of denial, as women always doubted men? Ah, what a maze of trouble, William thought, and there could never be peace in a world where there were such troublemakers as Jessica, a woman of no worth whatever, one could say, and yet a source of confusion and misery to them all.

A mile beyond the house Edwin stopped the car and jerked at the brake. He turned half around in his seat and faced them. "I am so stunned I don't know what to say. It's all utter fantasy. I don't know what she's talking about."

Elinor interrupted. "When she stood with hands on your shoulders that day in the hall, what was she saying?"

"What day?" Edwin asked, bewildered. "She's had a

95

way of putting her hands on my shoulders ever since we were kids. I always tried to stand out of reach."

"Why didn't you tell her to stop it?" Elinor asked in a hard voice.

"I didn't want to hurt her feelings—you always told us not to—" Edwin retorted.

Vera sat, silent, her head drooping.

"Had you any intimation," William asked slowly, "that she was in love with you?"

"I never thought of such a thing," Edwin said bluntly. "It's revolting," he added passionately.

He gazed at them, suddenly haggard. "How in hell am I going to prove she was lying? If you don't believe in me, who will?"

Vera turned her graceful head. "I believe in you," she said distinctly.

"Oh, Vera—" his voice broke.

"We all believe in you," William said in a practical voice. "I think Jessica has gone out of her mind. She's making things up. Maybe she thinks what she dreamed about is real. We had better just ignore the whole thing."

"Certainly," Elinor said. She recovered herself as he spoke and leaned to touch her son's shoulder. "It has nothing to do with you, Edwin. I do think simply that poor Jessica must have medical attention. I shall speak to Herbert and Bertha. Now drive on home."

They drove in silence, but who knew what was going on in the minds of those two, sitting in the seat in front of him? Yet long ago William had learned that the safest way to deal with the inexplicable was to ignore it until it became explicable. The subconscious mind worked beneath the routine of daily life, the blessed necessities of food and drink, fresh air and sleep and above all of work. What madness indeed might take place between human beings were there not the command of work to be done, the body to be fed and clothed! It occurred to him when they reached home to explain Jessica in this fashion to Elinor.

"Do you think it is mere idleness that afflicts Jessica? She has too much time on her hands—maybe she always did have."

"She wouldn't have so much time if she took care of the house properly," Elinor said tartly. "Herbert tells me she will not wash his clothes any more. He has to hire a neighbor woman to do them. And you remember he has bought two vacuum cleaners—that's more than you have done for me, William."

She looked at him with suddenly twinkling eyes.

"Herbert is a fool," William said.

Nevertheless this folly could assume vast proportions. Herbert, Elinor said, believed everything Jessica told him. He listened at night to her pretty voice making hideous disclosures and in the morning he stared at Bertha in a way that made her afraid of him.

"Herbert looks at me so, too," Bertha had told Elinor only last night. "I dondt like how he looks."

"Jessica is too clever for Herbert," Elinor now said. "He believes everything she says because she speaks good English and he never got beyond the fourth grade. Sometimes I think we had better send the whole lot of them packing, I don't care how long they've been with us."

"We must wait until after Jessica has had the baby," William replied.

"And," he added after a moment's further thought, "they work as well as ever. In fact, I don't know that Bertha has ever cooked better than she is doing and Herbert is certainly trying. He actually asked if I would like him to brush my shoes the other day."

So they would wait for the birth of Jessica's child.

Vera's visit lasted a week, and nothing more was said

about Jessica. In her calm way Vera planned her wedding, setting the date forward to early July instead of, as she had planned before, making it in September.

"Edwin needs me," she said simply, her eyes blue and calm.

And William, divining some lingering uncertainty in Edwin, suggested what he had only been thinking of, that Edwin should come into his law office after the honeymoon and get his apprenticeship through practice, taking his work at law school after a year, or possibly two.

"It won't hurt you to know something before you go to school again," he said to his son. Inwardly he felt it would do Edwin good to be self-supporting for a year or so after his marriage. Thus they united as a family to mend the breach that Jessica had made.

"WHEN is Jessica to have her baby?" Elinor inquired of Bertha.

Bertha shook her massive head. "I dondt know nottings—" she said stubbornly. "They tellt me nottings—*nichts, nichts!*" She and Herbert seldom spoke. The kitchen, which had been a companionable place, became a room of solitude and hostility. Herbert ate his food in the pantry, serving himself.

When Elinor asked Herbert he, too, shook his head. "Doctor can't seem to tell," he replied evasively. "Any time in the month, I guess."

The weeks went by and the child was born. One morning, however, Herbert did not appear for breakfast. A telephone call later in the day explained the reason.

"Jessica has been took," Herbert bawled into the mouthpiece. "I'm at the hospital. She had a hard time and I thought I lost her. It's a girl. Doctor says there can't be no more. He's tying her toobes right away."

"Oh, Herbert, that's too bad," Elinor exclaimed.

"It don't matter," Herbert said. She could almost hear him wiping the too ready damp from his face and neck. Herbert sweated easily, summer or winter, an emotional effluvium that had nothing to do with heat or cold. "I guess I won't be at work for a couple days," he added.

"Never mind," she said. Really it would be a relief. She put up the telephone and went out into the kitchen. Bertha down on her hands and knees was scrubbing out the oven.

"Bertha," Elinor said gently. "Herbert just telephoned. You have a little granddaughter. I'm so glad."

Bertha sobbed suddenly. "It dondt do me no good."

"Yes, it will," Elinor said, filled with pity. "As soon as she is big enough Herbert can bring her here to see me, and then you will see her, too."

"Herbert dondt let me," Bertha muttered, thick with tears. She inserted her head into the oven and reached for the far corners and her voice came out hollow. "Herbert, he hates me, now, too."

"Oh, Bertha," Elinor said impatiently. She left the room, and did not speak to Bertha again all day, waiting until William came home.

"They seem determined to hate each other, the whole lot of them," she declared. "I feel sorry for that poor little baby."

"A girl again," William said thoughtfully.

He was reassured, however, by Edwin's wedding. Bertha and Herbert responded to the family's crisis, a

99

wedding demanded co-operation. Winsten and Madge came with the children, Susan had come from college, and Ozark Pete, as William was beginning to call him privately, arrived the day before, at Susan's command.

The big house was full, there was no time for any but their own concerns, and William relaxed, a boon he deserved, for he had brought to triumphant conclusion his engagement with the city criminals. The three rascals whom he defended, not for their worth but for their rights as citizens, however mean, were discovered to be only minor in comparison to the real murderer, who was apprehended, through the confessions of the fat-faced man among the three. The prime criminal being safely in jail and destined for the electric chair, the three minors were out on bail, severely warned by William who promised them no further defense except upon good behavior. Now he was ready to forget evildoers and bask in the pleasant goodness of his family. It was June, the house was open at door and window, and his small grandchildren played outside happily. He was pleased by the deep devotion between Winsten and Madge, and not too much annoyed by Madge's air of triumph at having come to the wedding upon the eve of the birth of her third child.

"He can be born anywhere," she said recklessly, bursting into laughter. "It might be fun to have him born right here in his grandfather's house."

William merely smiled, praying inwardly that it might not be so. Meanwhile the weather reached perfection. Edwin had come home from college with honors enough to please his parents. So far as William could see, there was no cloud between the young man and Vera, and at the proper time the family set out for Manchester, where the wedding was to take place at two o'clock in the afternoon.

No, there was not a cloud between the two. Edwin

came quietly into the nave of the church with Winsten, his best man, as handsome young men as one saw nowadays, William thought, the minister approached from the opposite door in full regalia, and the organ, changing from its wistful strains of "Oh, Promise Me," until the solemn joyful wedding march, gave warning that he must with all others rise to his feet. Only Cousin Emma, because of arthritis, remained seated on the front pew with Vera's mother.

So William watched again the unfailing pageant of life, the touching powerful procession, his two small grandchildren, scattering rose petals before Susan in gold gauze as the maid of honor, the following bridesmaids in pink and ivory, and at last the tall white bride, so young, her hand upon her father's arm. William had been through it with Winsten and yet somehow this time he was moved more deeply. Vera had refused to believe evil of his son, she had stood by him steadfastly upon his word, a noble young girl, ready to become a noble wife.

He was somewhat disturbed in spite of himself, however, by the statuesque coldness of Vera's face. White as marble, she moved slowly forward, and she did not look up to meet Edwin's ardent eyes. Gazing now at his son's face, he wondered if in the strongly focussed, expectant eyes he did discern something like anxiety. Could it be that Jessica had indeed destroyed something between these two, even though there was not an iota of truth in what she had said? Were there even a trace of truth he could not have blamed his son. A boy growing always too quickly for himself is not to be blamed.

He remembered at this moment, most unwillingly, an incident in his own youth. He, William Asher, in love with the girl Elinor, had nevertheless been compelled to confess to her in the lovely and dreadful week before his marriage, that he had once been such a fool in his senior

year at Harvard as to let himself be taken by a gang of
college mates to a hideous house on the edge of Cam-
bridge, far from the Yard. What he could not confess was
that she herself was partly to blame, the long engagement
she had demanded, her gradually increasing yet always
delicate warmth, the weariness of their slowly approaching
wedding day, his fear of himself, lest the controls break
and he offend her at the very outset of married love, how
could he explain to the virgin Elinor these darknesses?
His experience had been ugly enough so that he fled the
place early and alone, but nevertheless there remained
something to be told, and Elinor had listened, as white
as Vera now was, and as hopelessly pure. He still remembered her forgiveness, the moment of his deepest
self-abasement, for years not allowed in his memory until
now suddenly it came back whole, his resentment increased because in spite of the years he had never let
her know she ought to share the blame with him.

He felt profound pain now for his son, and wondered
if at any time it would be possible to hint that Edwin
must never ask Vera to forgive him, even if what Jessica
had said had been wholly true, lest by asking forgiveness
he confirm her doubt of him.

Upon this he brought himself up with a start. The two
were making their promises while he was so unfaithful
to Edwin as to act in his thoughts as if Jessica had been
telling the truth instead of, as he truly believed, merely
the worst of falsehoods, to be explained only by the sort
of inexplicable madness that sometimes besets a woman.

Winsten put the ring from his vest pocket into his
brother's waiting hand and Edwin placed it upon Vera's
finger, speaking the ancient and beautiful words, and now
they were spoken, the two knelt to receive the benedic-
tion, the prayer for their lifelong faithfulness. William
had perfect confidence in the quality of his son, born to

be faithful to duty as well as to love. But would Vera make demands upon him beyond that which a man could bear? Jessica had cast a cloud upon them, nevertheless, he thought gloomily, a cloud even upon him because he would never know what Vera might do to his fine son, and he might have to wait for years to pass before he knew, and then only by watching Edwin, whether he held up his head in self-confidence as a man could do only when he was sure of his wife's approval as well as of her love. But if he saw Edwin's proud head begin to stoop, if he saw that dreadful downward look of the man betrayed by his marriage and wounded by his wife's superior purity, then he would know.

The wedding march burst forth with the peal of bells, and the two marched toward the open door, and Edwin held his head high enough. But Vera's face was still white and cold.

Elinor was sleepless. William, waking from what he realized was only light slumber, saw that although she had shut the door between their rooms, the door, shrunken with age, left a good half inch beneath it open and in this generous crack he saw light cast by the yellow lamp shade of Elinor's bedside lamp. Lying exactly as he had waked, flat upon his back, head thrust back, he listened and heard her footsteps prowling about in velvet slippers. He turned enough to see the illumined face of the clock upon the small table beside his bed. It was three o'clock, that dreadful hour at which the hidden worries of the day creep out like beasts of the night, to snarl and spread their poisonous forebodings. He sighed and got up, thrust his feet into his slippers and put on his bathrobe. He had left the cord of the belt in a knot and he fumbled at it, impatient, and then let it go as it was. He knocked at Elinor's door. There were times when she did not wish to have the door opened, and he had learned this early.

She did not now reply to come in. Instead he heard her inquiring voice, rather high, "Yes?"

"Are you sleepless?" he called back.

"Come in," she said after the briefest pause.

So he went in. She was lying now on her chaise longue holding about her a soft silk quilt.

"Can't you sleep?" he repeated, staring at her. Her long hair, looking silvery blonde as it had in her youth, was braided in two braids and these hung over her shoulders. Her face without makeup was white between them and he thought she looked exhausted.

"I keep thinking about Vera," she said abruptly.

"Why Vera?" he asked stupidly.

"Does she believe what Jessica said or not?" Elinor asked, not of him, but anyone.

He sat down on the end of the chaise longue. "Can we do anything about that, my dear?"

"I keep wondering."

He would have liked to go to bed, remembering the work piled upon his desk for the morrow, but he knew her tenacious mind. He had taught himself to turn off his own mind, he could delay further thought until he felt ready to begin it again, but she pursued conclusion without stop, although when she reached it, he reflected, she never thought again of that single pursuit. The answer, when she found it, was final.

"I am afraid of what Vera's thinking," she said gently.

The words, so cool, so absolute in their gentleness, brought him a violent shock.

"Will you never forget?" he demanded. "Haven't all these years meant anything to you? Haven't I proved my faithfulness?"

"Of course they do—of course you have," she replied, her voice, her eyes caressing, "but will Vera know?"

He saw what she meant, he thought gloomily. Vera was at the point where he and Elinor had been twenty-five and more years ago. It was Edwin's wedding night, alas!

"I thought it was all dead and buried decades ago," he groaned.

"It is," she insisted, "but don't you see that it has only begun for Edwin and Vera tonight?".

"Has that anything to do with us?" he demanded.

"They are our children and we want them to be happy."

"We've been happy—can't we trust them to find their own happiness as we have?" he urged.

She did not reply, she thought this over, there was reservation, he felt it, he saw it in the silence in the closing look of her face.

"I suppose only I understand how Vera might feel," she said at last.

"Come," he said with impatience, "after all these years, is there still something you have not told me?"

They looked at each other and the years faded into unreality. What was real was their wedding night when even in the midst of his hunger and ardor, he had seen tears in her eyes. She was so beautiful, the delicately strong, the exquisitely slender girl who was at last his own. Her pale gold hair that night was spread on the pillow like a wide halo, he had spread it so, marvelling at the length, the fineness, the living touch of it in his hands. In those days there was everything to know upon his wedding night. He had never seen her hair down, he had never seen the contour of her breasts, the shape of her waist, the roundness of her lips, the long grace of her legs, her narrow feet. He had never even seen her ankles bare. Absorbed and trembling, rapt in passion and wonder, incredible that all was now his, he had not seen her tears until the light from the lamp fell upon her face and he saw them shining in the blueness of her eyes.

He had fallen back. "What is wrong?" he demanded.

"Nothing," she had faltered.

"But something," he had insisted, and pausing, harnessing and holding back all his onrushing love, he had probed and questioned, had wrenched from her the truth that she could not forget this was not the first time for him, for there had been that other woman.

Why had he told her? If he had not been so utterly truthful he would have concealed the whole wretched meaningless episode, the college prank, to which he had yielded because of her intolerable delay, the act so suddenly repulsive to him even in the doing, so miserable to remember, which indeed he was determined to forget. He had explained all this again to her on his wedding night. She had seemed to understand. But now so many more years later he saw that she had not understood! And would not perhaps ever understand. It was a sacrilege to have brought into that magic hour of first love, yes, that holy hour, the folly which he had felt himself childishly compelled to confess to her.

"My God," he cried out now, "how I wish I had never told you!"

"Do you?" she asked. "Do you really wish you had not told me?"

"You have never forgotten," he accused her.

"I forget nothing that has happened between you and me," she replied.

"And not satisfied with never forgetting," he cried out against her, "you transplant your memory to your own son and his young wife!" He got up and walked about the floor. The cord he had not been able to tie was a nuisance again, his bathrobe did not stay together, he had to stop under the light to discover the mischief.

She got up automatically, then, and untied the cord for him, her thin fingers nimble and dexterous where his fumbled. She tied the belt securely about him and lay down again and drew the quilt to her neck. He accepted the service without thinking.

"Vera has grown up in a more sensible age than we did," he went on. "The war made women more sensible, at least."

"By sensible just what do you mean?" she inquired.

He was unwilling to analyze and then he did so, against his will. "I mean simply that man and woman cannot be judged by the same standards. That is as old-fashioned as Adam, but the truth remains ever new."

"Then you think Edwin is guilty?" she said too quietly.

"Guilty?" he repeated. "I don't know what you mean. If you mean is Jessica lying—yes, I do—that is, I think she is."

"You think she is," Elinor repeated.

"How does anyone know anything?" he replied, irritated. In some absurd far-reaching illogical fashion Jessica had woven even his abortive folly into the web which now caught even his son into its meshes. Had he not gone to Rose Schwenk's place, Elinor would not have believed Jessica, it would have been incredible that her son and his could have stooped to a servant girl, even though the girl was Jessica. But now!

And all this was taking place in this present year, this most modern year, the papers full of divorce and scandals, where sex was reckoned as only an appetite, scarcely to be confused with love. Here in his home, in Vermont, in a valley encircled by green mountains, he and Elinor were living in an age the world had forgot. Such was the power of love.

He turned to his wife, his face set, his jaws white, his teeth clenched, and he held out his arms.

"I will slay myself for you," he muttered. "I must have your faith as well as your love. I will not be betrayed by your distrust in me. For if you do not trust me, then all else is dust upon my head, ashes in my mouth."

His black and bitter eyes compelled her, she was overcome by his despair, and she rose instantly from the couch and went into his arms and he held her, his cheek upon the top of her head, upon the soft crown of her hair. No words—no words—only this, and let it be enough, at least for tonight, and at least for themselves in their generation. The young must learn in their own fashion, for no one could teach them. Love must be learned afresh by every human heart, newborn and alone.

"I want to go and see Jessica and her baby."

This was Madge at breakfast, surrounded by her young, a proud madonna, her husband on her right hand. Elinor was late, a most unusual accident for which William was grateful when he entered the dining room promptly at half past eight. He had not dared to open her door, but listening outside he had heard no sound.

The sun was bright after a light rain just before dawn, a gentle roll of thunder introducing the sudden cloud. Herbert was zealous with buttered toast for the children, and Madge was announcing her intention to him as William entered the room.

"Good morning," William said. He sat down and received the sticky kisses of his grandchildren, who had been instructed, he felt sure, by their mother, to kiss their grandparents morning and night without fail, and at any time between. Madge was a demonstrative wife and mother, believing that kisses and endearments were the cement of family life.

It was impossible not to appreciate the picture she made as a young and blooming mother, his daughter-in-law, although he averted his eyes when Winsten picked up Madge's plump little hand and held it to his cheek. Winsten was uxorious, and this was repellent, but he was glad his son was happy. Both parents adored the sight of their children kissing their grandfather.

"That's right, darlings," Madge cooed. "You must always love Grandfather."

"Yes, indeed," William echoed sincerely enough but conscious of the coolness of his words and tone in contrast to Madge's rich enthusiasm.

Herbert did not answer Madge's announcement. He left the room murmuring about more hot toast, and Madge went on comfortably now to William. "I do feel I should show some interest. After all, Jessica grew up in this house, and this is her first child. Then, too, I might be of help. It is very sad that she will not let Bertha even see the baby. I might be able to say something."

"I shall be glad if you can raise Bertha's spirits," William said. "It may do Jessica good to see someone so entirely normal as you are, Madge. I confess I cannot understand Jessica."

He pondered whether he should tell them of Jessica's extraordinary outburst about Edwin and then decided that he would not. Even though it was all in the family, one never knew how Madge might take it. There was no jealousy between the two brothers, he believed, but Edwin now had a wife, and granting that Vera was altogether different from Madge, William was not sure that this removed her from the possibility of jealousy, her own or Madge's. He was not used to having two daughters-in-law, nor was Madge used to having a sister-in-law—beautiful and young, whose figure as yet was unspoiled. He imagined that Vera would never allow her figure to be spoiled, whatever the number of her children, and this in itself might be a source of jealousy one day, for Madge

109

was the mother type who believed that babies should be breast-fed, and she would think it indecent to consider the contour of a woman's breasts more important than their use for motherhood, or indeed for any other use at all. Winsten, William thought, glancing sharply at his son, looked completely fatuous, a thin intense young man, devoted in fatherhood. What sort of husband was he? Well, Madge had made him whatever he was. Madge was inexorably maternal, her soft massive love absorbed all about her. It was only with the greatest firmness that William himself refused to be absorbed. He loved his grandchildren, sticky though they were with morning marmalade, but he refused to consider them more than a sideline in his life. He was determined to be something more than a mere grandfather, however Madge might view him. It occurred to him that perhaps the only way Winsten could be his young wife's lover was to embrace her first as the mother of his children. A revolting possibility, William thought, averting his mind from the scene. He finished his breakfast hastily, making only a few ordinary remarks and grunting occasionally when the children put a question to him. Then he got up.

"I shan't wake your mother," he said to Winsten at the door. "Ask her to telephone me when she gets up."

He left them with a propitiatory smile, a kiss tossed off his moustache to the children, and was glad to get away. Herbert had made a quick change and was the chauffeur again, immobile and silent at the wheel. William was going this morning only to Manchester, the city office being in the usual summer slackness. It was odd but true that city crime took a moderate vacation in the summer, too, growing brisk again in the sharpness of autumn air.

The green hills were pleasant, the sunshine spilled over into the valleys and he wondered if he should speak to

Herbert merely in good humor and decided against it. There was something threatening about Herbert's tight small mouth this morning. So he sat silent and at peace, putting out of his mind the difficulties of human relationships, and meditating upon the gratifying aspects of the law, where all was according to pattern and precedent and one knew exactly what was right. A pity such patterns could not regulate the minds as well as the actions of men and women! He enjoyed the approach to the town, and noticed the attack of tourists, school teachers on a holiday by the busload. The car slowed and Herbert chose a side street and they drew up before the old red brick mansion which years ago William had made into his first law office, and from which he would not have departed now for any cause whatsoever, although he had almost no local practice any more. The older he grew the less change he wanted in his life. This alone made Jessica a menace. Remote as she was, a contemptible creature, yet the irrationality of her uneducated mind created a force which could destroy a rational and innocent universe however small, and that universe his own. He considered again the dismissal of Bertha and Herbert, a clean sweep, removing his household from the fatal orbit within which entirely by chance they were being drawn. For he did not believe for a moment that they had heard the last of Jessica. Yet constitutionally he distrusted clean sweeps.

The morning passed quietly at his desk and he was only uneasy at noon when he allowed himself to realize what he had been aware of all along, that Elinor had not telephoned. He ordered his lunch sent in from the nearby hotel and decided that he would not call her. That she had not called him meant either that she was still asleep, which he could not believe, or that she did not wish to call, in which case she had better be left alone. Long ago he had learned that it availed him nothing if his impa-

111

tience compelled him to find out her reasons before she chose to reveal them.

He allowed the day to pass, granting himself only no delay after five o'clock. To his astonishment, when he went out to the car he found that the driver was not Herbert but Winsten.

"It's a surprise, I know," Winsten said, reaching to open the door. "Get in—it's been a queer day. Herbert had to go home. Madge thought he should."

William got in. "What's wrong now?"

"Madge wanted me to tell you alone on the way home," Winsten said.

He steered his way carefully among clumps of tired tourists, waiting to get into returning buses. "Madge feels terribly sorry for Jessica. She thinks we ought to do something for her immediately."

"Well, well," William said, "let's get it over with."

The scene, reconstructed from Winsten's cautious narrative and propelled by his own dry occasional questions, was clear enough. He and Madge had taken the children with them this morning and had driven to the farmhouse. There they had found everything wrong. No one had answered their cries or knocks, and at last listening they heard the baby crying upstairs. Madge could bear it no longer. She tried the front door and found it unlocked.

"Winsten, you stay here with the children and I'll go up," she had commanded.

"What about the dog?" William interrupted.

"We didn't see the dog then," Winsten replied.

Madge had gone straight upstairs, although the steep stairs were difficult for her. She went to the door from which the baby's crying came, and then she heard Jessica weeping in low moaning wails.

She tried to open the door, but this door was locked.

112

She shook the handle. "Jessica!" she cried, "let me in. It is Madge Asher. We've come to see you."

Then she heard the growl of the dog, the loud bass roar. "Jessica!" she cried again.

"I can't let you in," Jessica called back, her voice all broken with sobs. "I can't hold the dog."

The dog sounded vicious enough to make Madge pause indeed. She went down the evil stairs again and out into the yard, where Winsten was waiting with the children, and told him what Jessica had said.

"You get into the car and stay with the children. I'll go up," he said.

She obeyed him, for now she was honestly afraid. It was too strange. Why had Jessica locked herself in with the baby and the dog in that upstairs room? Or had she? Perhaps Herbert had locked them there. She got into the car with the children and Winsten searched the yard and found a heavy stick.

"Do be careful," she begged from the window of the car.

"I'm not afraid of a dog," he retorted.

He climbed the stairs and rattled the handle of the door. "Jessica!" he shouted. "It is I, Winsten Asher. What is the matter in there?"

She stopped her sobbing, and he supposed she must have taken the child in her arms, nursed it perhaps, for its crying stopped abruptly. Only the dog continued its horrible hoarse growling.

"Open the door," he commanded.

"In a minute, Mr. Winsten," she said in her usual sweet voice. "I just have to tie the dog."

What was this, Winsten asked himself. Could she not have tied the dog before? He heard her talking to the dog in her light coaxing way.

"Now stop, Pirate. It's a friend. You needn't be excited.

113

It's Winsten. Don't you remember Winsten? He was always my friend."

A moment after that she opened the door and he saw an incredible sight. She stood there, quite composed, the child at her breast. Behind her was the dog tied into a huge kennel which stood between the twin beds.

"Come in, please, Mr. Winsten," she said gently. "I am not strong enough to go downstairs yet, and I keep Pirate up here with me while Herbert is away. There are so many tramps, especially in summer, and they all seem to know that I am here alone."

Her meek voice, her pure accents, calmed his astonishment, even his horror, for the dog was a dreadful sight, its meaty jaws slathered with foam, its red eyes rolling. Still, he could understand that she was afraid.

"Shall I call Mrs. Asher?" he suggested.

"Oh do, please," Jessica said almost gaily. "I am so glad she has come, it's very kind of the family."

So, much bewildered, he had gone downstairs again to fetch Madge, who was astonished, too, when he told her, and they left the children for a moment, locked in the car, and went upstairs together. Jessica had sat down in a rocking chair and the dog had ceased to strain against the leather thongs which tied it into the kennel, although its jaws still dripped and its baleful eyes still glowered.

"Do come in, Mrs. Winsten, dear," Jessica said warmly. "I was just sitting there crying all by myself I was so lonesome. I didn't recognize your voice. I couldn't hear you clearly else I would have let you in at once. I have always to tell strangers at the door that I daren't let the dog loose."

It was all reasonable enough, except that it seemed absurd and unreal.

"The front door was open," Winsten said.

Jessica looked vexed. "That's careless of Herbert! I beg

him to lock the house when he leaves in the morning but he thinks I am just silly. He has no imagination. He cannot think how it is with me here alone all day, and now this child—"

She looked down at the child as it suckled, her eyes almost hostile, and Winsten had his first quick distrust of her. For gazing at that innocent face, the eyes closed now, the lips relaxing, Jessica asked in strange abstract wonder, "How could this child be born? I shall never understand."

Madge was touched. "Oh, my dear," she remonstrated. "You must not talk like that. When men and women love each other, babies always come."

Jessica looked up at Madge standing above her like a kindly goddess of fertility.

"Ah, but I don't love Herbert," she said clearly, coldly.

Madge turned to Winsten. "Go downstairs, dear, and see to the children. I shall be quite all right. I must have a talk with poor Jessica."

So unwillingly Winsten had gone downstairs and Madge stayed and she repeated their talk faithfully afterwards to Winsten when they were driving home.

"It is very wrong not to love your own husband, Jessica," she had said.

"Oh, I know it is," Jessica sighed. "I try and try."

"Did you never love Herbert?" Madge inquired. She pulled up a small chair and sat down and took the baby in her arms. Poor little creature, she thought, it looked like Herbert and was quite ugly.

Jessica drew her dress over her breast and leaned back and closed her eyes. "It's all so—disgusting!" she whispered.

"What?" Madge asked.

"To have to be alone with Herbert here in this room, night after night—when I don't love him."

Madge was shocked. "Why did you marry him?"

"Mr. William Asher said I must."

"My father-in-law?"

Jessica nodded, and large tears welled beneath her golden lashes and slipped down her pale cheeks.

"But why?" Madge demanded.

"I cannot tell you," Jessica cried. "Oh, I must never, never tell!"

She did not tell, she would not tell, she could only weep hysterically in a convulsion of sorrow. She clung to Madge with both hands. "Oh, you must never, never ask me, promise me," she cried. "You must never mention it even to Winsten. Only Edwin knows. Edwin knows everything. But Mr. Asher doesn't know that Edwin knows. Edwin was like my brother. Oh, he *is* my brother —we'll never change to each other."

Frightful vistas opened before Madge. Jessica was too pretty, she had always been too pretty, and older men could be very strange.

"But did he—" she began.

"Oh yes, yes, yes," Jessica cried in a rush.

"Tell me this," Madge said sternly, "how long did it go on?"

"Oh, years," Jessica said desperately. "When I came back from the convent I was only seventeen. I couldn't help giving in then, could I? It went on and on."

The dog began to growl suddenly and Madge gave a start.

"He won't hurt you," Jessica said. "It's only men he hates. I've taught him that."

The baby slept on peacefully in her arms and Madge could have cried. Poor little thing, what chance had it here in this house? What a tangle life could be!

"Please don't cry, Jessica," she said mildly. Her own life had been so happy that she had no notion of what to do now. She felt the firm universe, the little warm universe which was her own, begin to crumble about her. If Winsten's own father—

She got up and laid the baby on the bed and put a bit of the counterpane over it. "I shall have to think what to do, Jessica," she said. "I want to help you but now I don't know how. I have to think of the family first."

"Oh, yes," Jessica agreed humbly. "We must always think of the family first. I quite realize that."

She got up and stood waiting, looking so quiet, so sad, that Madge was overcome with pity in the midst of her daze. "Poor Jessica," she said simply. "It must have been awful for you, living there."

Jessica's eyes filled again. "I can't forget," she whispered.

Madge nodded and unable to speak she went downstairs and closed the front door and crept into the car. . . .

"I think it best to tell you exactly what happened, sir," Winsten said. He had taken the long road home, to give them both time. Now, his eyes upon the road, golden in the late sunshine, he did not turn his head even to glance at his father's profile.

William had pished and pshawed while the narrative went on. Now however he was in the stillness of profound wrath.

"This is just enough," he declared between set teeth. "Jessica is insane. There is no doubt of it. The idea, the very idea—"

He swallowed and coughed and choked. Winsten slowed the car and thumped him on the back. "Take it easy, sir."

"I know you wouldn't believe such a ridiculous hallucination," William said hoarsely, still stifled. "I'm not so sure about Madge. Women are infernally ready to believe the worst about men when it comes to sex. Even your mother—" His cough seized him again and threatened to strangle him.

"Here, here," Winsten said, pulling up to the side of the road.

"Choking—on my own spittle—" William gasped, purple in the face.

Winsten waited, thumping him gently and rhythmically on the back until he had control again of his wind.

"Well," William said, wiping his eyes, "that was a performance! I don't know that I ever had such a thing happen to me before. But I was never so angry before. Does Madge think—?"

"I don't know what Madge thinks in her heart of hearts," Winsten broke in wearily. "She's a creature of instinct, as all good mothers are. When she's pregnant everything is exaggerated."

"You don't mean she really believes I would demean myself with a servant girl!" William shouted violently.

"She doesn't believe anything exactly," Winsten said doggedly. "She just feels with Jessica somehow."

William shut his mouth firmly and folded his arms, and sat stiff and silent. "Let's get home," he muttered after a moment. "I'm going to talk to Herbert."

The contamination of Jessica in his household might be dreadful, indeed uncontrollable, if Madge were allowed to spread her feelings about. Something had to be done. He was not afraid of any woman, certainly not of his own daughter-in-law, and he would simply stop the whole trouble at its source, which was Jessica. Jessica could not be allowed to go on like this and he would tell Herbert so. Herbert was at least a man, and Jessica's husband.

He got out of the car at his own door and upon the terrace saw Susan and Pete; they were playing a childish game of some sort together, rubber balls attached to long strands of rubber and wooden bats. Each of them had such an instrument and they were laughing loudly. They did not see him and he passed them by. It was odd that Pete did not go back to his business, his garage in the Ozarks or whatever it was. He would be glad when Susan's wedding was over, too. Let them all get married and go away and leave him and Elinor in peace.

Herbert at the door took his hat and cane.

"Come into the library, Herbert," William said sternly.

"The dinner is just on the boil, sir," Herbert suggested.

"Never mind," William said in the same voice.

"I'd better warn Bertha," Herbert said.

William stalked ahead into the library and shut the door. He sat down in the highbacked oaken chair at the end of the long table of English oak and waited. In a moment Herbert came in soft-shod and closed the door and stood against it, his large face pale.

"Yes, sir?"

How could he begin, William asked himself, how could he repeat to Herbert the vile and foolish fantasy which Jessica had woven? Begin he must, and he did so firmly.

"Herbert, my elder son and his wife went to see Jessica today in the kindness of their hearts."

"Thank you, sir—" Herbert whimpered under his breath.

"While there," William continued sternly, "Jessica told a complete falsehood to my daughter-in-law concerning events she declared had taken place while she was in my house."

Herbert's head drooped, his fat face began to quiver.

"I could take legal steps for defamation of character," William continued, "and I would do so except that I believe Jessica to be mentally ill. I demand that you have a doctor examine her at once."

Herbert's face disintegrated, his eyes ran with tears,

his tiny mouth trembled between his great cheeks, his chin shook like a dish of jelly.

"It's that black dog, sir," he sobbed.

"The dog?"

"Yes, sir. She don't let me come near her—weeks and months it's been. The dog stays between her and me day and night."

"Do you mean to say she keeps the dog there all night when you are at home?" William inquired, aghast.

"She keeps the dog because of me, sir," Herbert faltered. "She ain't afraid of no man—just me."

"What do you do to her?" William demanded.

Herbert pulled a large clean handkerchief from his pocket and wiped his face. "Nothing, sir, except I want my rights."

He folded the handkerchief neatly and put it into his pocket. Then he looked at William humbly, his face glistening with sudden sweat.

"Sit down," William ordered.

Herbert sat down on a corner of one of the heavy chairs and continued to look at his master with eyes piteous but dogged.

"Explain yourself," William commanded him.

Herbert cleared his throat and leaned forward slightly. "As man to man, sir," he began—

And upon this William, his eyes fixed upon Herbert's pallid and glistening face, saw unfolded before him a scene as old as man and woman.

The man, who only happened to be Herbert, advanced nightly upon the woman whom he had made his own with her consent, given for what reason could not be imagined, and nightly the drama repeated itself, Jessica's delicacy, her fantastic imagination, her thwarted longings, her melancholy inheritance shaped in remote ages in the Black Forest of Germany, concentrated now into a single blind determination. She would not yield to this man, she the woman. Oh, she had yielded at first, half laughing, flouncing at him, "Leave me alone, you dirty beast!"

He had left her alone then sometimes, cunningly trying to arouse desire in her by ways he knew, ways he had tried before on other women, ways he had heard men talk about—

"Don't touch me, *schweinehund!*" she had screamed. "I am not like that."

He had been cautiously patient, knowing that good women did not give in all at once. But what does a man do when a woman never gives in? What does a man do when a woman bites and scratches him so that he had to hold down her hands and thrust his arm against her throat so that she cannot raise her head and then must mount her hard so that her kicking legs and thrusting feet do not wound him in his tenderest parts?

"I ask you, sir," Herbert said, the tears starting down his cheeks again, "what do I do?"

"I cannot imagine your wanting to—to compel your wife against her will," William said, sickened to the soul.

"What for does a man marry?" Herbert asked, astonished. "A man pays, don't he? He gives her bed and board, so to speak, and everything else beside. I've give Jessica everything she ast for—"

He ticked off again on his stubby fingers what he had given her, the Beautyrest mattresses, the washing machine, the two vacuum cleaners, the almost antique furniture, the gold-edged mirror, the new blankets, the refrigerator, the electric stove, at last the carpet, yes and carpet even on the stairs.

"What do I ast back? Just my rights," Herbert said. His humility passed from him suddenly. William saw a man remembering his wife whom he was determined to possess.

"What's more, I'm goin' to have my rights," Herbert said, heavily.

"How do you propose to get them?" William inquired, his voice grim.

It was useless to explain to this male that there was no getting without giving. The subtleties of sex were beyond Herbert's comprehension. The delicate lessons which he himself had taken so long to learn Herbert could never grasp, nor even their necessity. Perhaps for Herbert they were not necessary. To take might be enough for this molecular soul surrounded so massively with body. But ah, Jessica was another material. William had mercy enough in his heart suddenly to be sorry for Jessica. He caught a dim glimpse of what it might mean to be a woman.

"I'll take my rights," Herbert said. His small mouth pursed into a tight knot. "First of all, I'll get rid of that dog."

William sighed. "Why don't you handle the matter a little gently, so that she won't suspect? Ask Pete to take the dog back. Say that it is getting too fierce with the child and you would be obliged if it could be taken away. Then Jessica will not blame you so much."

Herbert stared at him. "It's a good idea, sir. It takes a lawyer, I guess, to think of how to do things." He hesitated. "I wisht I could do it now, tonight."

"Why not?" William replied. "You might ask Pete at once. He will be leaving perhaps tomorrow."

Herbert got up. "Thank you, sir—Bertha will wash the dishes, I guess."

"Go now," William said. He did not want Herbert about the dinner table tonight. "Madge said your wife was in a bad way this morning. Get home to her. I'll speak to Susan. They can go with you, tie the dog in the car, and get their dinner somewhere on the way home."

"Thank you, sir."

He waited for Herbert to leave and then he went out to the terrace and there found Elinor with Susan and Pete. The game was over, Susan was shaking cocktails and Pete was lounging in the most comfortable chair.

"Get up, you big bum," Susan said cheerfully to her betrothed. "Don't you see my father?"

Pete got up, grinning. "Didn't know this was your chair—"

"It isn't, particularly," William said. He paused to kiss Elinor's cheek and took another chair.

She said, "I heard you and Herbert in the library, and I didn't come in."

"Jessica is in a bad way," William replied. "Herbert feels he must go home at once. Susan, he has a strange request to make but I concur in it for reasons I will explain later. He wishes that Pete would take away the black dog."

"Now?" Susan's dark eyes were large.

"At once," William said firmly.

He glanced at Elinor to see if her face betrayed the slightest change of knowledge. He saw nothing. The twilight fell upon her lovely hair and placid eyes. Madge might be honorable enough, after all, to say nothing except to Winsten, and his own son he could trust. As soon as possible he himself would tell Elinor the whole miserable fantasy, once the dog was gone, once Herbert had a chance to assert his will. He felt guilty in strangely hidden ways, that he was, so to speak, delivering Jessica over to the male, but perhaps that was what she needed. She had been spoiled all her life, catered to, indulged, nobody had ever made her do anything, beginning with gentle old Heinrich, and even Bertha with her sporadic slaps and tantrums, and certainly Cousin Emma. They had all made far too much of a child who though she happened to be pretty and vaguely talented was after all doomed, or destined, rather, to be nothing but a servant. Let Herbert beat her if need be, once and for all. He did not want to talk to Elinor until this was over. Elinor would somehow prevent it.

Herbert drew the grey car in front of the terrace a few minutes later and sat immobile.

"Well, Pete?" Susan inquired.

"I don't care," he said amiably, and so the two went off, and at the same moment Winsten came down, preventing William from being alone with Elinor.

"Where is Madge?" Elinor inquired. "I'm ashamed that I've slept all day. But I felt tired after the wedding."

"Madge isn't feeling quite herself," Winsten replied. "I have told her to go to bed."

"Oh dear," Elinor said, "is it, do you think—"

"I don't know," Winsten said, "it may be. We'll soon see."

His thin young face was worried, the perpetual father, William thought, not without relief that Madge could not appear.

"The trip this morning was too much for her," Elinor said.

"The children have been fretful this afternoon," Winsten replied. He poured himself a cocktail. "Where are Susan and Pete going?"

"Herbert wants the black dog taken away tonight," William said significantly. "I talked with him about Madge's impression of Jessica this morning. He thinks the dog has an unhealthy influence on Jessica—has thought so for a long time."

"How strange," Elinor said in surprise. "I wouldn't have suspected Herbert of so much subtlety."

"It may be only a notion," William said quietly.

Winsten said nothing. He stirred his drink slowly, his eyes downcast.

"Don't worry about Madge," his mother said. "It would be rather nice having a baby born here the way you all were."

"I'm only thinking about my job," Winsten said. "I ought to telephone the first thing in the morning."

"Well, not until morning," Elinor said comfortably. "Let's go in to dinner."

It was well toward midnight before William heard the car come up to the terrace. He had not gone to bed, pleading papers, and he had sat alone in the library working after Elinor left him.

"I shall sleep with one eye open," she had said. "I don't like Madge's looks. I think something is going to happen before dawn. Winsten has called the doctor. He's made a reservation in the hospital, at least." This was after she had been upstairs to see Madge.

"That's better," William said absently. "I hate nurses in the house—always did."

She laughed softly, and kissed him. "You dried-up old lawyer," she said. "Babies mean nothing to you, I do believe."

"I like them when they're washed, properly dressed and looking like human beings."

"You always acted as though you had nothing to do with ours," she accused him.

"My part was somewhat vague," he admitted.

She shook him slightly. "Such talk," she scolded, but lovingly.

He smiled up at her and when she bent to kiss him again he held her down for a moment, his hand on the back of her neck.

"Have you been quite happy with me?"

"On the whole, yes," she said round and clear.

"I never forced you—against your will?"

He thought he caught the slightest flickering of her golden eyelashes. "Not really—"

"No, now, Elinor," he demanded.

"Oh, let's not talk about things at this late date—"

"Indeed we will," he said with sudden anger. "Come, sit down. Now when did I ever force you against your will?"

She sat down, opened her blue eyes very wide and began to take down her hair, pin by pin, and braid it before his eyes, growing younger by the minute as she did so.

"All right, stupid, if you don't know by now. Of course you forced me, not by raping me or anything so silly. Still, plenty of times a woman doesn't want—but she does it anyway, because if she doesn't the man gets huffed, irritable, cross the next day with children, and it just isn't worth it—"

He stared at her and felt something collapse within him.

"Elinor," he stammered. "Elinor, you didn't—"

She gazed at him rebelliously. "Yes, I did, and you have made me tell something I didn't want to tell and don't want to tell, and now that I've told you, you are going to get angry with me. How unreasonable and illogical and emotional and ridiculous men are! You want romance, all the time, it's all to be love-making and sex, but it has to be to your tune and when you say so, and if the woman doesn't happen to be ready all the time, any time, and remember the bull and the cows, if you please, the bull always waiting and ready, damn him, but he has to wait on the mood of the cows as any farmer knows, and it's only the human female who has to deny her very

126

nature and pretend and pretend, and then you can't believe the truth. Oh, you men, you must have nature itself the way you'd like to have it, you can't and won't face the truth—"

"Elinor!" he shouted, "have you lost your mind?"

She flung her braid over her shoulder and gave him a glorious and bewildered smile. "No," she said softly, "and I feel wonderful! I do believe I have wanted for years to say that. Now I've said it." She put her clasped hands on her breast. "Thank you, William, for giving me the chance."

She took a deep breath, not a sigh, but the breath of freedom, and he stared at her in stupefaction. "Why didn't you say it years ago if you wanted to?" he demanded.

"I didn't dare," she said strangely. "I used to be afraid of how you would feel."

"And you're not afraid of me now?" he said rather sadly.

She shook her head and the waves of her soft hair parted on either side and fell over her ears. "No, I suppose because the children have grown up, I can't think of any other reason."

"I don't understand you," he confessed. "In spite of loving you and you only all these years I don't understand you."

She rose and went over to him and putting her arms about him she pressed his head into her fragrant bosom.

"It was often completely right and wonderful," she whispered. "Most wonderful of all, it still is. Better really, because now it's just for you and me. It's so nice that God has arranged for younger women to take over the worry of having the babies."

He buried his face between her breasts. "Oh, Elinor,"

he muttered, forgiving her for everything. "I'll never have time enough with you."

"All the time there is," she said cheerfully. She bent to kiss him firmly but briefly upon the lips. "Good night, don't sit up all hours."

She pulled herself away and detected a speculative look that he permitted to creep into his eyes and she laughed. "No, no," she said airily, "not tonight, not with this house full of children, Madge likely to be taken to the hospital at any moment, and that dreadful dog coming back—"

She shuddered and went away quickly, pausing at the door to say one last word, "I do thank you, William—"

"Don't thank me," he muttered, going back to his papers, and forcing his mind away from her. All that stuff she had poured out, there was no telling how much of it was truth, and how much of it was thought up on the spur of the moment. There was something of Jessica in every woman.

Nevertheless he felt quite sleepless, and when he heard the car just before midnight, he tiptoed to the front door which was standing open. Madge had not gone to the hospital, and the upstairs was dark except for the night light in the hall.

"Be quiet, you two," he said in a low voice when the car stopped.

"What's wrong?" Susan asked with something just under her usual voice.

"Madge isn't feeling well," he replied. "What's that?"

For between the two of them they were dragging an immense dark body out of the rear of the car.

"It's the dog," Susan said. "Pete had to kill it."

"What an extraordinary day!" William muttered under his breath. "What are you going to do with it?"

"Put it here behind the lilacs until tomorrow, Pete," Susan said. "It will smell up the car."

Pete did not reply. He dragged the huge corpse along the ground by the forepaws, flung it behind the lilacs, and then came up the steps looking depressed. "I never thought I'd kill a dawg."

"Come into the library," William commanded softly. "What on earth happened?"

They tiptoed after him and he closed the door.

"I want a drink," Pete said. His dark face was somber and Susan looked at him with troubled eyes.

William went to a small cupboard in the panelled wall and took out a bottle of whiskey and three glasses. He poured a small amount of the liquor in each and they drank slowly.

"Well?" he inquired.

"You tell it, Susan," Peter said.

He sat with his knees apart, his head hanging while she talked, his full lower lip thrust out.

"Jessica was asleep when we got there," Susan said. "Herbert went upstairs alone first, of course. He looked in and then he came down again. 'She's got the dog loose in there,' that was what he said. 'I don't dast to go in,' he said. So of course Pete said he would go up. We all went up, Herbert last."

She told it well, struggling, as William could see, with her own horror. They went up the stairs without making any noise, thinking, she said, that they would take the dog away without waking Jessica or the baby.

"Does she always let the dog loose when you're late?" she asked Herbert.

"She keeps him on a long rope, as a reg'lar thing," Herbert replied.

But Jessica had waked at once. "Is that you, Herbert?" she called.

"Answer," Susan commanded him.

"Yes, it's me," Herbert said in a placating mild voice. He held the door. "I tried to come before, Jessica, but I heard the dog loose."

"You can't come in, Herbert," Jessica called back. "I have the dog loose on purpose."

Herbert turned his big pale face toward them. There was a naked electric light in the ceiling blazing down on them.

"Now what'll I do?" he begged.

"Tell her we're here to get the dog," Susan said.

The dog was growling horribly just inside the door. They could hear its rasping breath drawn in after each growl.

"Miss Susan is here with Mr. Peter," Herbert said placatingly. "They've come for the dog, Jessica. Mr. Peter wants it back again."

Jessica did not answer. They listened and heard nothing but the growling of the dog.

"Let me open the door," Peter said. "The dawg knows me." He flung the door open but the dog sprang at him. Standing on its hind feet, it was as high as his shoulders and he grappled with it, holding its jaws shut with one hand.

Herbert closed his eyes and leaned against the wall, moaning, but Susan sprang forward and dragged the dog's hind legs so that it fell on the floor.

"Smart girl," Pete gasped. "Hold 'em down. I'll choke the life out of the damn beast."

"And that is what he did," Susan said in the library, facing her father steadfastly. "I held the dog's hind legs and Pete choked him dead. And then I heard Jessica. She was saying over and over, 'Kill them, Pirate—kill them all!' I was so angry when I heard it, and I yelled at her. 'You shut up, Jessica!' That's what I yelled. It was like a roomful of crazy people, Herbert crying out loud and Jessica saying that over and over and me yelling at her. She was sitting up in bed all dressed up in a silk nightgown and a fancy bed jacket, pink sheets on her bed, if you please. Only the baby kept on sleeping."

"What did you do when the dog was dead?" William asked. His mouth felt dry as leather and he sipped the whiskey again.

"Pete dragged the body down the stairs and we stuffed it in the car and came home," Susan said.

"Yeah," Pete said in his heavy voice, "and I never thought I would kill a dawg. I always liked that dawg. I never should of brought it here. I should of left it at home where it belonged. She had that dawg all strung up tense like and ready to kill anybody. Why, the way that dawg was tonight it would have eaten Herbert alive. Lucky for him we went along."

"I suppose you saved his life," Susan said, "if it was worth saving. I doubt it. I despise men who cry. I never cry myself."

"Let's go to bed," William said. "I am exhausted."

He was waked the next morning late by Elinor's cool hand on his forehead.

"Wake up, Grandfather," she said gaily.

He dragged himself upward out of sleep. "Don't tell me Madge—"

"A little girl, named Elinor," she said too brightly.

"Another girl," he exclaimed, waking up.

"Too many?" she inquired.

"Depends," he said, yawning. He got up and shuffled into his slippers.

She paused at the door and blew him a kiss. "You look tired. Would you like to stay in bed this morning? Herbert's not here."

131

"Oh no, I'll get up," he grumbled. "Herbert's not here, eh? Susan tell you about the dog?"

"She came in my room last night and waked me up to tell me," Elinor said. "Terrifying, wasn't it? I'm glad it's dead. Jessica will be better, I do believe."

"I don't know," he mumbled from the bathroom.

She did not hear him. She was already on her way downstairs, her spirits high because of the new baby. A girl was what she had wanted, he could see. His own spirits sank strangely. This was not going to be a good day. They had not seen the end of Jessica, not by a long shot.

It was the middle of the morning, however, before he knew the worst. After breakfast, not having seen any of his children, he withdrew again into his library, taking care not to look out of the window to see whether the dog lay behind the lilacs. Susan was still asleep and Pete was probably the same. The young these days seemed able to sleep all day, a sort of escape, he felt, from the insoluble problems of the times. No one knew how to stop war, corruption in government was monstrous, women went crazy and dogs went mad, therefore the young slept.

At eleven o'clock when Elinor had just left for the hospital to see Madge and her baby, he himself declining to go before the baby was twenty-four hours old and the first rawness off, he heard a scream in the kitchen. The back window of the library opened upon the kitchen garden and the morning being warm he had opened it to make a current of air. He was therefore able to hear Bertha scream loudly again and then again. He flung down his pen, but before he could get up she came rushing into the room in her stocking feet as she always was in the kitchen, especially in summer when her feet swelled.

"Mr. Asher, sir, oh, Mr. Asher—"

She sobbed, her face was purple.

"Well?" he said sharply.

"Herbert, sir, he's on the phone, Jessica—she's gone something awful—"

William picked up the receiver on his desk and heard a strange noise.

"Herbert!" he shouted.

"Oh, Mr. Asher," Herbert moaned, "please can you come quick?"

"I cannot," William said firmly. "I must first know what is wrong."

"It's Jessica, sir—can you hear her?"

"I hear a dog barking," William said.

"That's her!" Herbert shouted. "She's down on her hands and knees going round and round the room. She's actin' like a dog, she's stark ravin' crazy. I don't know what to do. And the baby is hungry. I can't get her to feed the baby. She tries to bite it. I can't stop her goin' round and round barkin'—"

"Oh, my God," William cried. "I'll call an ambulance. Good gracious! Watch her, Herbert—"

But when he had called the doctor and told him and the ambulance arrived, it seemed there was nothing for it except to go with it himself, for the country roads were inexplicable and the quickest thing was simply to leap in beside the driver. A nurse and an interne with a strait-jacket sat in the back by the stretcher.

He rode in silence while the lovely summer morning shone down peacefully from heaven upon the troubled earth.

"That was some dog lyin' there dead under them lilacs," the driver remarked.

"It is to be buried this morning," William said in a distant voice. It would be impossible to explain all that had happened, and he felt too exhausted inwardly to make an attempt. It was simply not to be understood.

"That's the trouble with living near a highway and keepin' a dog," the driver said amiably.

"Yes," William agreed, too exhausted to explain.

"It must have took a truck, though, to kill that dog," the driver suggested.

"I suppose so," William said vaguely and then uncomfortable.

The driver gave up and was silent until they drove up to the farmhouse.

William got out, followed by the interne and the nurse and the door was opened by the driver. At the foot of the stair William paused. "Herbert?" he called. The bedroom door opened and they could hear a strange low growling from upstairs. Herbert came out with the baby in his arms.

"She's quieter," he whispered. "She's layin' under the bed."

William turned to the nurse. "You had better go up without me. She knows me and might get excited."

He was uncomfortable indeed. What if Jessica should recognize him and renew her charges? He sat down in the small parlor, now ill-kept and dusty. Herbert had made it a place to change his clothes, and his shoes and undergarments were scattered about, a piteous place, he thought, looking about at the touching effects that Jessica had tried to create, a little world for herself in which she had nevertheless gone mad.

They were bringing her downstairs now, in a white coat of some kind, the sleeves tied around her. He caught a dreadful glimpse of her as she passed the door, her head down slung, and her jaw slavering. She was muttering in her throat, a rasping guttural growl, and they passed the door without her lifting her head. He rose and stood by the open window and when they put her into the ambulance, she snapped at the interne's wrist suddenly, and he slapped her.

"You'd bite, would you?" he said not unkindly. He strapped her down upon the stationary cot within and the nurse took her place. The driver climbed into the seat and then shouted, "Ain't you comin' back?"

William shook his head. "I will stay and see how things are here and the man can drive me back later."

The driver nodded and the ambulance rumbled away. The house was still. There was not even the sound of Herbert weeping. William went upstairs after a moment and found him sitting in the chair, rocking back and forth, the baby asleep in his arms. The room was frightful. Some sort of human battle had taken place. The bed clothes were tossed over the floor, the pictures had fallen from the walls, glass broken, and the curtains were torn from the windows. In the midst of this wreckage Herbert sat in the rocking chair, the baby in his arms, rocking back and forth and the child was placidly asleep.

"How did you feed it?" William asked stupidly.

"I mixed some milk and water and sugar and fed her with a spoon, sir," Herbert replied. He seemed calm but exhausted. "Do you want me to drive you home?" he asked.

"What about the baby?" William countered.

"Now that she's full she can just sleep in the back seat," Herbert said.

So with no more words they went downstairs, Herbert put the child in a rolled blanket in the back seat of his worn car and they went slowly away from the house.

"You'll understand I can't come back for a day or so, sir," Herbert said. "I'll have to get the baby into a home somewhere."

"Certainly," William said. "But wouldn't this be a good

135

time to have Bertha retire and come here and take care of the child?"

Herbert's immense white face took on a look of rock-like stubbornness. "I'll never have her in the house, sir, not while I live."

"But Bertha has done nothing," William protested.

"I don't know what she has done nor what she hasn't," Herbert said darkly, his little sad eyes on the rutted road. "All I know is that Jessica couldn't abide her and so I can't. Something she did to my girl, and I shan't lay eyes on her in my house."

"Does that mean you want to quit your job?" William asked.

"No, it just means I don't want her in my house," Herbert repeated.

"Is it not Bertha's house?" William suggested.

"It's to be Jessica's and mine as soon as the old woman dies," Herbert declared.

William was silent, there was no fathoming Herbert's mood. He would be glad to get home.

"Or again," Herbert said half a mile later, "it might be them nuns. Jessica was never willin' to give herself up to herself. There was somethin' about nature that she thought was dirty and that's the nuns. Still, it was Bertha sent her to the convent, where her father never wanted her to go. She liked her father, Jessica did. He was good to her."

William could remember Heinrich very well, a disorganized kindly man who without Bertha to direct him would certainly have ended as a drunkard or a beggar. But that was perhaps the tragedy of women like Bertha, the managers to whom the weak turn, upon whom they cling, and whom unfailingly they hate, and this, too, could not be explained to Herbert.

"Well," he said vaguely, "one never knows. I suppose

the first thing is to get Jessica well again, if it's possible."

Then Herbert said the incomprehensible thing. "She ain't sick, sir, she's just tryin' to win."

"Win what?" William asked.

"What we went through last night."

He would like to have cried out not to be told what had gone on, but he saw it was necessary for Herbert to tell him. Sooner or later Herbert would insist upon telling what had taken place in that room after the guardian dog was dead, after Susan and Peter had gone away and there was no one left to stand between the man and the woman. It was plain enough as he told it. Even so soon after childbirth the endless war of the ages between male and female had burst into battle in that lonely room, far from any human habitation, so that Jessica screaming and crying could be heard by no one. No, and Herbert, too, was not heard, his slow temper rising at last to crisis when he knew that she was defenseless, and no one could hear the bellowing of the bull, alone at last with the weaker female. Jessica did not yield. She leaped from bed to floor, she clung to the curtains, struggling to throw herself from the windows, but he had nailed them shut. The curtains fell about her and she hid in them until he tore them from her. She clung to the table, to the beds, until he wrenched her hands away, pounding upon her knuckles with his clenched fists. He beat her with the rung of a broken chair at last until she fell writhing upon the floor, screaming with pain, and still as tireless, thin as she was, as though she were made of twisted wires. He imprisoned her beneath his vast body there upon the floor and held her down, his hands clutching her wrists, his tight mouth pressed upon her turned cheek, his loins fastened upon hers.

"And all the time," he said mournfully now in the morning light driving carefully along the road so that the sleeping baby would not be jarred from the seat, "all the time I was takin' only what was my rightful due."

William listened, fixed in solemn horror. There was simply no way to explain to Herbert that what he had done was worse than murder.

"When it was all over," Herbert was saying, "I lifted her up and laid her on the bed. I thought she had fainted and I was scared. I went in the bathroom to get her smellin' salts. She always had smellin' salts like Miss Emma. When I came back—" his chin began to quiver and he cleared his throat. "When I came back into the room she was on her hands and knees on the floor, swingin' her head low, and when I spoke to her, she—barked, like the dog."

William drew a deep sigh. Another five miles and they would be home.

"It is all incomprehensible," he said at last, "quite, quite incomprehensible."

But he had a dreadful fear that if he really tried, he could understand, and to understand was, for the moment, simply too much for him.

When he got home he looked involuntarily for the carcass of the dog. It was gone. Susan and Pete had buried it, then! Now perhaps there would be peace. He went upstairs to wash his hands and change his clothes for no particular reason except that he wanted to look as well as to feel differently, a change surely for the better. On the stairs he met Susan and noticed that her eyes were at once remote and luminous. He made no reference to the dog.

"Where is your mother?" he inquired mildly.

"She is in the herb garden," Susan replied and went on her way.

When he was properly changed into an old suit, newly

cleaned and comfortable, he went in search of Elinor. She was as Susan had said in the herb garden, a square of greenery in the midst of the kitchen garden behind the house. She was on her knees, choosing slowly and with care a small bouquet of herbs, designed he supposed for the delectation of the meat she had planned for their dinner. He walked toward her, lighting a cigarette and pretending an amiable leisure.

She looked up. "Well?"

"Well, Jessica has been taken to the hospital—in a straitjacket." He said it gently, low enough so that Bertha could not hear. Elinor would have to tell her.

"A straitjacket!" Elinor cried in high concern.

He described the dreadful morning and she listened, frightened and yet unbelieving, as he could see. She knelt there on the ground, protesting in silence while he told her what he had done.

"Somebody had to do something," he said in final irritation. "Even Herbert agrees to that. The doctors will decide whether Jessica is or is not insane. I hope she is. Insanity is the only possible excuse for all that has happened. If she is not insane, she must be a devil of malevolence."

This made an impression, he was grateful to notice. The sparkling protest faded from Elinor's eyes.

"Oh dear," she sighed. She sniffed the herbs and rose to her feet. "I wish I knew whether it's the right thing."

"For the present it is," he said firmly. He himself felt a strange relief in the thought that Jessica was safely locked up.

"I suppose so," Elinor said. "Of course they have all sorts of ways of curing people now—even if she is insane."

"Yes," he agreed, and then very guardedly, he asked, "How's Madge?"

"Perfectly normal," Elinor replied. "That is, she is well

139

enough physically. I thought she seemed a little queer with me. I suppose she is just tired."

He felt his cheeks grow hot. "I am tired myself. I have had just about enough of queer women," he said with unusual energy. "If Madge feels queer I had rather not hear about it. How is the baby?"

"I'm sorry you're tired," Elinor said. "As for the baby, she is simply adorable, the prettiest of all the babies."

"Then I am glad she is named after you," he said gallantly.

She flashed him one of her looks, fully appreciative, a little humorous, meaning isn't it rather late in the day for this sort of speech. He raised his eyebrows and noticed that her skin still stood the sunshine remarkably well. She had no wrinkles, not even a delicate tracery under the ivory surface. He felt gratified that he had been able at least until now to keep her life serene enough for beauty.

"I LOATHE men who weep," Susan said with unutterable loathing. "Thank God Pete is a real man. I would hate Herbert, myself, if I were Jessica, I swear."

It was evening, and William was waiting for dinner. Elinor was in the kitchen, Bertha had retired to her attic room upon hearing the news of Jessica, and Susan was setting the table.

"Ah," William said to encourage Susan and yet not to commit himself. It was all very well but there could be extremes either way. "Is Peter not coming for dinner?"

"No," Susan said. "He decided to go home this afternoon."

"Nothing wrong?"

"Not if you and Mother behave," Susan said firmly.

He avoided this portent. She wanted something and so it was she, he very well knew, who had sent Peter home. She wanted him out of the way while she took her parents in hand. How well he recognized the signs! He got up and sauntered toward the door.

"You'd better help your mother with the dishes after dinner, Bertha is prostrated."

"There it is again," Susan replied. "Getting prostrated! People are so soft."

And if anyone looked soft, William thought, gazing at her, it was this luscious creature who was his daughter, this girl with the tender air, her large brown eyes fringed with black lashes uselessly long and thick, her slender round figure, hinting plumpness that was like his own mother's, a voice as deep and soft as slumbrous music. But that was the fashion of girls these days and it all meant nothing. He had not the slightest idea of the real Susan since Pete had attached himself in his singularly lackadaisical and desultory manner to the family. Yet apparently it was to be permanent.

He seized upon an instant's daring. "Are you really going on with this preposterous marriage?"

Susan folded three stiff linen table napkins into fanciful shapes. "That is what I want to talk about tonight. I am glad that Bertha is prostrated. We'll have perfect privacy."

"Wait until after dinner," he begged, pausing at the door. "My digestion is not what it used to be. Peace, please, at our meal."

He left her, and somewhat heavily he went outdoors

141

and walked back and forth upon the terrace, suspending thought. Long ago he had learned the trick of self-suspension, a defense against criminals pervading his inner life. He had been compelled to learn how to send them off into the outer air, their evil faces fading away like Cheshire cats, in order that he might return whole to his household to play with the children, to examine the defects of a reluctant furnace, to read a book he had laid aside the night before, or finally and most important of all, to make love to his Elinor. Now in the long summer twilight he exercised his habit and felt a refreshing inner quiet steal forth. The garden was lovely in the dusk, the early summer flowers bright against the stone wall. It was weather for roses, the only flowers whose name he infallibly remembered. Whatever happened within a man's house, the walls stood, the trees grew high and flowers bloomed.

But the foundations could be shaken nevertheless. The evening went on and Susan was merciless. The meal was pleasant, delightful so far as the food went, he made tentative veiled references to the exhaustion of his day, and yet he perceived that Susan had no intention of sparing him. The young were single-minded, they thought only of themselves. Glancing at his daughter occasionally between moments of enjoyment of a lamb curry that was really superb, he muttered within himself and strictly to himself that he might as well enjoy his dinner, for what was coming afterwards was inescapable. He knew the look of inexorable determination upon Susan's beautiful mouth, he had seen it first when she was less than a year old, in conflict then as now with him, beginning, he recalled, with the day upon which he had insisted that she eat her spinach. She had not eaten it. Instead she had brushed the dish to the floor with one swift movement of her then fat left hand. The hand now was very pretty, slender and well-kept, the nails coral red, and upon the third finger he saw for the first time a diamond ring, a solitaire of size. When she saw him looking at her hand she flashed the diamond in his eyes like a lantern.

"Like it?"

"I've seen others," he said drily.

"It's very nice," Elinor said, hastening to make amends for him by generosity.

"Where did Ozark Pete get the money for that?" he grumbled. There was no use being delicate with Susan. Girls nowadays did not know what delicacy was. Jessica had modeled herself on the young ladies of another day.

"You'd be surprised how much money you can make in a garage," Susan said complacently. "Besides, we bought it on time."

"Oh, Susan," her mother exclaimed.

"What?" Susan asked.

"But your engagement ring! On borrowed money!"

"I didn't want the small size," Susan said.

"Get what you want, get what you want," William said.

"Okay, Dad—"

"Even your English is corrupted," he grumbled. "A college education can't stand up against a garage, I suppose."

He saw he had gone far enough for the present. Her dark eyes burned with fury upon his face. He shrugged his shoulders slightly. "I won't quarrel at the table. There'll be no punches pulled later, though."

"None," Susan promised.

He rose from the meal and without conscience he left the table and dishes to the two women, and proceeded to smoke a quiet pipe in the east parlor. There in that peaceful place, all children and servants removed, he reflected upon the strange human phenomenon of modern

143

times, the tough guy Peter, and millions more like him, uncivilized and ignorant, a magnificent body and no brain, or if a brain, then so well concealed beneath mannerless behavior and uncouth speech that it might as well be nonexistent. He felt sorry for his own sons, Winsten, the young father, molded in a pattern outworn, and Edwin, the intellectual, who could not survive, certainly, unless law prevailed. If ever law broke down beneath the assaults of revolution, inevitably it would be Peter who was the revolutionist and never Edwin, and certainly not Winsten, and Edwin would be liquidated. That was the modern word for murder. Winsten might be allowed to live if he conformed, and he would conform, fearful for his wife and his children. Edwin would never conform and so he would be killed. William savored the harsh old-fashioned word. Killed was the truth of it, and liquidated was the lie. Peter might hate to kill a dog, which was his slave, but he would not hate to kill a man more intelligent than he, more educated than he, who at some future and perfectly possible time might try to uphold the tables of the law when Ozark Pete wanted them broken. And could Susan not understand this possibility, and in the day to come would she stand beside the brute or would she choose the blood to which she was born? He did not know. A woman could not be counted upon when it came to love.

Somber thoughts upon a summer night!

"And why, pray, are you sitting in the dark?" Susan demanded in her velvet voice, so soft and deep and yet unrelenting.

"Thinking," he replied.

She did not ask what thoughts. Instead she went about turning on one light after another, until the large quiet room was blazing. Probably she did not care what he thought.

"I don't like to hurt you," Susan said sweetly in the midst of light. She sat down on the couch, leaned her elbow upon her hand and curled her feet under her. There in her apple green frock, short-sleeved and round at the neck, the full skirt billowing about her, she looked a child, a dreaded child, William thought, too well loved, too much indulged, too clever, too adorable.

Knowing through the experience of her years that she liked to arouse concern, he avoided this direct attack.

"By the way, I meant to ask, where did you bury the dog?" He acknowledged to himself the morbidity of the question, the desire to know once and for all that there was a definite end to the despicable creature.

"Pete took him out into the country," Susan said. "He threw him down the old marble quarry."

The old marble quarry was filled with water to an unknown depth. Long ago, in a generation past, it had been used as a swimming hole by the sons of farmers until a boy had drowned so deep that no dragging could bring his body to the surface. The quarry had then been forbidden.

"I am glad that the beast was not put into our ground somewhere," William said.

"That dog was too big to bury," Susan said indifferently. "Pete said it would have taken him half a day to dig the hole. Still, he was angry about it—a good dog spoiled."

"A savage beast," William said decisively.

Silence fell, light and tense, necessary to be broken quickly.

"What do you plan that will hurt us?" Elinor asked. She had come in while Susan was turning on the lights and had taken her usual chair. Now, contrary to habit, she was smoking a cigarette while she sipped her coffee.

"Perhaps we cannot be hurt," William said.

"Oh, yes, you can," Susan declared, "but it can't be helped. I know you are disappointed in me, but I guess you understand that I am not going to finish college."

He had feared it. She had hinted as much at the seashore and when she came home he had noticed a finality in her behavior, a definite return, complete in intention. Neither he nor Elinor spoke. Susan tossed her short hair from her face and toyed with her ring.

"I shall marry Pete right away," she said.

"Oh, no," Elinor began, but Susan put up her hands.

"Mother, I don't want a wedding."

"Oh, Susan," Elinor cried.

"Pete would look silly—I know it. No, don't say a word, either of you. I know every word you would say. I know what you think of Pete. I can see him with your eyes every time you look at him. That's why I sent him away today. I want to wrestle with you alone. I know how you feel about him, I tell you."

The dark eyebrows leveled in a furious frown above her brown eyes.

"And you don't care?" Elinor asked.

"I do care," Susan said. "But I shan't let it change me toward Pete. I shall marry him."

"When?" William asked with dry lips.

"Any day, the first day we can," Susan said.

Silence fell again, and this, William thought, was the end of their children! For this, one built a house and made it home; for this, one worked and denied pleasure, waked in the night—he remembered how the child Susan grew thirsty always in the early hours after midnight, when he was in his first deep sleep. Night after night he had got up out of bed, groaning, to fetch the cupful of water, taking a small share of responsibility that Elinor might be spared, and yet it was not small for he was of the tense mind that once waked could not easily sleep again so that the brief service drained away from him an hour or more of rest. Year after year it went on, and a cup of water set at her bedside did not answer the purpose. She needed to make sure of his readiness and his presence. It was more than a cup of water.

"Tell me why you love Peter?" he asked in a coaxing voice. "If I could understand that, I might find it easier to have you leave us. For you are leaving us in a very total sense when you marry him."

He caught a hauntingly childish terror in Susan's eyes as he spoke these words.

"Oh, no," Elinor said quickly, "she can always come back. Marriage needn't be permanent nowadays. People get divorces."

He was amazed at this speech. Elinor had always been merciless toward divorce, always, she said, the woman's fault. She refused to believe that any man could not be held, as women put it, if the wife tried.

"I shall never divorce Pete," Susan said. "No matter what he does, it's permanent."

"Tell me why you love him," William repeated.

The question embarrassed Susan strangely and she did not reply. She bit her red lower lip, she examined her nails.

"He is not at all the sort of young man we had imagined you would choose," William went on. "I don't mind so much your leaving college unfinished. I realize that time is shortened these days for the young. With another war threatening it is quite natural, perhaps. But Peter is foreign to us, and so in a measure he must be to you, or so we imagine."

He kept his voice calm, his manner judicial and as far as possible unprejudiced.

"After all, we know you better than you think," he went on again, to give her plenty of time. "I don't believe in the Oriental fashion of choosing the persons whom one's children marry, and yet one does get to know one's child."

She said in a small choked voice, "You get to know me in a way—maybe you do. You know I don't like liver and onions, you know my favorite color is green, that I like to play tennis and don't like mathematics—that sort of thing. But you don't know what I am thinking—and feeling."

Her voice failed and she swallowed hard against tears.

"There are things we cannot know unless you tell us," he agreed gravely. He longed to reach out his hand to her, draw her to his knee as he used to do when she was a child, to stop her tears. But she was a woman now. Another man might do that but not he.

And Elinor sat silent, lighting one cigarette from another. Did she understand, ought not she to understand? He cast her a reproachful look which she caught and rejected. Manage this your own way, her eyes said. Well, he would. Susan could not be entirely remote from the child he had known and loved. She had not been too complex. She had been a direct child, ready of temper, quick with affection, not nearly so complex for that matter, as Edwin. She had never had his dark silences. It was only since Pete had come that she was changed.

"Where did you meet Peter?" he inquired and was shocked to realize that he had never asked the question before.

"At a dance, a blind date—"

It could happen, he reflected, as she went on with her story, in such times as these when all classes were churned together by war. Pete had come back from the Pacific, and before he went home he had stopped to see a friend, a buddy, in Poughkeepsie, a town boy whom Susan had met through her roommate, a nice boy who was going to

Yale. Pete had fought beside him upon a distant island and he had once saved Pete's life.

Susan laughed now in the middle of the story. "It ought to have been the other way around. Pete is so huge, and Eliot is so small and—oh, exactly so! His father is the Episcopal minister but he's not the least like most minister's sons, although I guess he is going to be a preacher, at that. Anyway, Pete was barging up one of those hills on Okinawa, all ready to make a hero of himself when Eliot, who was scared to death—says so himself—was sneaking up behind, sheltering behind Pete, really, holding his rifle ready to shoot at anything he saw, and of course he saw the enemy first and potted him."

Her voice was suddenly normal and her eyes dried. "Pete will never forget that. Eliot comes half way to his shoulder and Pete can swing him off the ground with one arm."

She was amused.

"But you don't care for Eliot," Elinor said quietly.

Susan put back her hair with both hands, restlessly. "Oh, who could? He's such a shrimp. Pete's strong—if you could have seen the way he caught that dog! It was like fighting a bear. He clenched his fist around its jaws and bent its head back until I could hear the bones crack."

"Susan!" Elinor cried, shuddering.

Susan looked at her mother with strange eyes. "That makes you sick, doesn't it, Mother? It doesn't make me sick, though. That's the difference between your generation and mine. It's what makes me have to love someone like Pete. With him I let go, don't have to care how I talk or what I do. What you two can't seem to realize is that everything has changed. The world isn't what you thought it was—or what you told me it was. It's another world and nothing can stop that, and it's I who have to live in the world. Pete knows what I mean. He says it's

149

only toughness that counts now and being able to fight for yourself. He's right. All the old soft stuff is gone."

"Yet Eliot—" William hinted.

"That was only an accident," Susan said quickly. "It doesn't change anything. Eliot says himself that he didn't plan it, he was scared to death. He says now he doesn't know how he did it, and he wasn't even thinking of Pete."

She leaped to her feet and walked about the room, swinging her wide green skirts. "It's such a rest to me to be with Pete. He doesn't care about anything—manners or small talk or any of the pretty-pretty stuff."

"He doesn't even care about being clean," Elinor remarked with caustic.

Susan turned on her. "No, he doesn't! It's not important to him. He likes dirt. I know what he means, too. When you've been bathed every day of your life and shampooed and scrubbed and made to wipe your feet when you come in and put on overshoes when you go out, dirt is wonderful! I tramped into his house with as much mud as I liked. If I wanted to bathe, I took a bath, if I didn't nobody cared. I could eat any way I liked, anywhere I liked, anything I liked, I could talk or not talk, swear if I wanted to—that's Pete's way and I like it."

"You have never really told us about Peter's home," Elinor said.

Susan looked at them, one and then the other, doubting, as William could see, whether she could trust them enough.

"Tell us," he urged, but gently.

She took the step against doubt and earnestly they tried to follow. "It's a shack of a house, you would say," she began, "but there are plenty of rooms, they kept building as the children came."

A wooden house lost in a forest of trees, two miles away from the highway and Pete's garage, a rough hillside farm, crops scraped from the earth by antiquated machinery, so that the children had little enough to eat and yet somehow on the energetic air and the pure water they grew tall and strong, though without a pound of flesh to spare, six boys and two girls. But Peter was the youngest of them all, so that the dilapidated house was empty when she went there, except for the father, the mother, and one of the sisters whose husband had been killed somewhere in Burma, which they thought was the name of a town, and the sister's children, three of them, all boys.

The house was one story, a string of rooms, the main one in the middle, the living room, dining room and kitchen all together, a long, ramshackle room full of broken-down furniture that was worn to the shape of big lank bodies, the sinking chairs comfortable with quilts and milkweed cushions. There was no yard, a small vegetable garden came up by the house on one side and the fields on the other, and chickens and several grey geese ran over the warped wooden porch floor.

At first Susan had thought the house filthy, but as she stayed she discovered that it was clean in its fashion, without paint, the mattresses on the beds of fresh corn husks, or, since she had the spare room, of feathers. There were no books except the family Bible and a few comics, nobody thought of reading, there was no music except that which Pete made upon his guitar when he felt moved, and a bath was to be had in the brook a quarter of a mile away or in a wash tub in the woodshed. Old Mr. Dobbs talked of electricity but none of his family believed he meant it or cared whether he did. Mrs. Dobbs cooked on an old iron stove and washed the clothes outdoors with water heated in an iron pot over burning logs.

And yet, Susan said, she had liked it. It was peaceful there, the trees tall and silent, the mountain water clear, and no need to talk unless one felt like it. Pete's sister, Maryanne, was sad, but she went on living, dealing with her children swiftly and cleanly. She loved them heartily, and could be angry with them as heartily. There were no barriers between any of them. You always knew where you were with each one of them, and they were all strong and lean and healthy. Learning was not necessary, life was simple and easily lived. They admired her when she cut wild flowers and put them in a pitcher, even though none of them thought of doing it. In the evenings they sat together on the porch, not talking or else talking, if they wished. Nobody cared.

And what she could not tell her parents here in the east parlor was that in that mountain setting love itself grew deep because there was nothing else. To love or hate, to wake or sleep, to live or die, these were the simple alternatives and one made one's choice. The complications of civilization were as though they had never been.

"My generation is tired of civilization," Susan said at last in a voice strangely old. "We can't understand why we must do all the things we are told to do, even to die for something that is beyond our comprehension. We are tired of being pushed around. Well, up there in the mountains, I won't be pushed around. I'll just live, and with Pete."

They listened to her in utter stillness, amazed, wounded, confounded. Elinor put down her cigarette, her hand trembling.

"It isn't even back to the gutter," she said in a stifled voice, "it's choosing the gutter you've never known. It's rejecting a civilization. You aren't even modern enough to understand. But why, but why—"

She was not asking a question, she was crying out the mystery she could not comprehend.

William went to her side and took the trembling hand. "Don't grieve, my darling."

Susan whirled upon them, her eyes flaming. "Oh, you two, what do you know? Only something that is dead and gone. I'll be safe with Pete, do you understand? Whatever happens, he'll keep me safe. He's tough, he's strong, he isn't afraid of anybody. He's got fists and he's ready to fight."

"Oh, my God," William whispered. "Is life as simple as that?"

He turned away and unable to resist an escape he went on into his library and closed the door. There he sat down and put his head in his hands. His daughter's words had made the tomb of all in which he had believed. To have fists, to be ready to fight, to hurl one's self up a hill against an enemy, any enemy, the folly of such simplicity crushed his heart. And so where was intelligence fled, and who had killed in this generation the daring of the spirit, the courage of the mind? Would there ever again be the resurrection of human truth? Wherein had he failed as a man, and Elinor as a woman that their child, their treasure, could so choose to hide herself in animal retreat? Susan was as foolish as Jessica, her dreams as vain, her faith as surely to be lost.

He got up and began the long pacing across the floor which marked the thinking process in his most abstract cases of the law. The child's reason was still there. Confused in her emotions, entangled by the subconscious fears of this generation at the endless prospect of wars ahead, a fear which now concerned women as much as men, women whose whole foundation must be in love and home, Susan still possessed her sane mind. If he could separate her for a time, even a brief time, from Pete, if they could all go away for a holiday somewhere, she and Elinor with him, go perhaps to England, where he had been told the young were steadier, older in the age of the nation than they were here, then she might yet be saved. She was too childish to choose now the course of her events. He made up his mind swiftly. He had business always waiting in England, he would make it imperative and insist that they leave at once, immediately, tomorrow if need be. And if she refused to go, he would compel her. His long dark face set itself in grim lines, the look that criminals had learned to dread, and he opened the door abruptly and faced his beloved foe.

"We are going to England," he announced. He stood there, dangling his pince-nez in his right hand. "I shall telephone for reservations on the *Queen Mary*. The sea voyage will clear our minds and give us time. We'll go to England and see whether the young men and women there are thinking in terms of fists and fights."

He looked from one surprised face to the other. "I don't ask for agreement. I shall demand obedience. We need perspective, all of us. I need perspective on you, Susan, for at present you appear a fool. The world is not so hopeless as you think. You have somehow happened upon a low level but there are others. Not all young men are Ozark Petes, thank God. Your brothers are proof."

Susan drew up the corner of her full mouth in a sneer. "Those two?" she muttered. "Do you call Winsten a man? He's a papa, just a papa—"

"Hush," Elinor said in a violent whisper. "Here he comes." It was indeed Winsten, returning from the hospital. He stood in the doorway, looking a little haggard, smiling at them with wan lips.

"The children have been good?" he inquired. He had put them to bed early, before he went.

"I haven't heard a word from them," Elinor replied. "Have you had dinner?"

"I dined in Manchester," Winsten said. He came in and sat down and lit a cigarette.

"How is Madge?" Elinor inquired. Someone had to ask the necessary questions. William stood where he had stopped, and Susan was pouting.

"She is in excellent shape. The doctor says we may go home at the end of the week," Winsten said gratefully. "They are getting her on her feet tomorrow. Seems strange, but everything is strange nowadays. We are all doing things we thought were wrong yesterday."

He smiled his wan smile again, caught a triumphant look upon Susan's face, turned to William.

"Have I interrupted something?"

Susan got up decidedly. "Nothing! I am going to bed. That's all. Just that and nothing more, my friends!"

She caught her circular skirt in her hands and danced out of the room on noiseless feet, and William watching her understood perfectly that she had no intention of obedience. He stiffened himself, his back straightened and he felt the angry blood rush dangerously through his veins. This was the sort of thing that brought blood pressure to the danger point, the technique of the young for hastening the death of the old. He forced himself to relax, breathing deeply, not heeding the hospital conversation going on between Winsten and his mother.

"Don't you feel well, William?" Elinor asked after a moment or two.

"Yes, yes," he answered impatiently. "Don't mind me. What were you saying, Winsten?"

"That it is fortunate I was born just when I was,"

Winsten said earnestly. "I escaped the last war and I'll be too old for the next one."

William got to his feet. "It's been an exhausting day, I think I do feel tired." He hesitated, remembering suddenly that now he would be leaving Winsten alone with Elinor, and Winsten with his usual sense of duty might feel it necessary, if his mother expressed anxiety, to repeat the absurd stuff that Jessica had said about him to Madge. Then he felt weariness creep over him like a pall.

"Good night," he said abruptly, and bending he kissed Elinor's cheek and felt her hand reach up to his face. Enough was enough, he thought, climbing the stairs, and today more than enough. It was a wonder he had strength to earn their bread.

Some time in the night, in the deep night when he was so sunk in sleep that Elinor's hand upon his face, smoothing his cheek, seemed only a dream left over from their earlier parting, he was impelled to waken. He heard her voice summoning him from afar.

"William, wake up, darling—William—William—"

"What—" he muttered, staggering upward out of the abyss.

She sat down on his bed, her silvery braids hanging over her bare shoulders. "William, are you awake?"

"Yes—yes—"

"No, you're not, poor thing. Oh, William, try!"

He hauled his consciousness out of the dark, hand over hand, opened his eyes wide by force and stared at her painfully.

"What's wrong?"

"I nearly didn't wake you," she whispered, "then I thought I must. I can't take the responsibility alone."

"Eh?" he demanded.

"Hush," she whispered. "Come to the window, William. Not a sound, mind you—"

He got out of bed and she seized his hand and they stole to the window and she parted the curtains.

"Look!" she whispered.

The light of the moon shone down upon the lawn in a pale mist. There in the driveway he saw a car, Pete's car. The young man was waiting motionless beside it.

"There is a light in Susan's room," Elinor said. "I have heard her moving about for the last half hour. I heard her go up and I knew exactly what was happening. I knew that Pete's car would pull into the driveway just like that. It is four o'clock."

He started impetuously for the door but she clung to him. "Wait—wait! It was such a beautiful idea that we go to England. But it is no use, don't you see? England can't do anything for her, William, nor for Pete. For us, maybe, yes indeed, but nobody can do anything for them, William, don't you see?"

"You aren't going to let her ruin her life!" he whispered hoarsely.

She put her arms about his neck. "We must let her go, William. We must just let her go and maybe then some day she will come back. If we try to stop her she will die before she'll come back."

He was too perplexed to refute what she was saying. What indeed if she were right?

She drew him gently back to the open window and they stood, waiting, and there hand in hand, their hearts beating with the sorrow that only the aging know, they watched the old, old play unfold itself, as it had for thousands of years. The front door opened softly and Susan came out, lugging two bags. Pete took them and put them in the back of the car, they moved noiselessly together, shadowy figures in the mist, they embraced and clung

157

for one long instant, then they climbed into the car and slowly the car crept over the gravel of the drive and passing through the gate faded away into the night.

He became aware then of Elinor's trembling. She was weeping! He took her into his arms, pressing her close. When had she wept before? Not for years! He was frightened, and he hated Susan. Let her go—let them all go, so long as he held the beloved woman who alone was his.

"I don't know why we ever had children," he muttered fiercely, his own throat constricted.

He felt her strangling her tears, choking back her sobs, struggling against breakdown. "Oh, cry," he begged. "What does it matter with me? Do cry, my darling!"

She shook her head and pulled away from him slightly. "I don't want—to—to cry. It's too devastating—now—at my age."

"Nonsense!"

"No, I know." She wiped her eye on her ruffled sleeve and swallowed once or twice. "I wonder—" she said after a moment.

"What do you wonder?" he asked, all tenderness.

She shook her head again and bit her lips and went on.

"I wonder if we'll ever be able to tell them that we watched them go—and let them!"

He smiled a bitter smile. "It would break their hearts. What, not oppose them? It would spoil all the heroics."

She laughed trembling heartbroken laughter. "I suppose you're right. We'll never tell them." And turning to him suddenly she threw herself into his arms and hid her face against his neck and cried desperately.

It was becoming clear, William told himself, that Herbert was not what he had been. Usually he enjoyed the long ride to New York, especially in the spring when the dogwoods spread through the woods a foam of white. Now, however, the ride was more often than not an ordeal. Herbert, once so stolid and calm a driver, was becoming erratic and reckless. William, complaining yesterday to Elinor, had blamed the parkways.

"Once Herbert gets on the parkway," he grumbled, "he seems to think he can pass every car in sight. Fifty miles doesn't satisfy him. His rate is sixty, if he thinks I am asleep he gets as high as eighty. We've been stopped half a dozen times in the last year."

"It's not the parkways," Elinor said. "It is Jessica. He had me call the doctor at the asylum last week and ask if Jessica wasn't well enough to come home for good, so they can bring the baby home before she gets any older. She's almost three years old now, and she doesn't remember any home but the orphanage. It does seem a shame."

William was reluctant to talk about Jessica, although during the years that she had been put away, there had been talk, of course. He considered her dangerous, remembering what she had said to Madge, and though he had heard no more of it, Winsten and Madge seeming the same when they came home for brief visits, now no more at Christmas since the fourth child, a boy, had arrived. Still, they met once or twice a year, and he continued to feel an unconquerable reserve toward both Winsten and Madge, even when nothing was said about Jessica. If she were mentioned Madge showed only a mild interest, her children absorbing her entire attention and continuing as the sole theme of her conversation. He did notice, William told himself, that she was no longer so insistent upon the children bestowing upon him kisses of dutiful affection.

"What did the doctor say about Jessica?" William had inquired.

"He says that Jessica may try it for a while at home, if she wishes to do so."

"Does she wish it?" he asked.

"That is what we don't know," Elinor had replied. . . .

The car swerved dangerously around a curve and he cried out, "Herbert, slow down!"

Herbert slowed down to an aggravating crawl but William did not speak again. The crawl would last only a few minutes. He allowed himself to be absorbed in his papers and the speed crept up. When a sharp siren blew, William rejoiced to see a state policeman. Let the fellow deal with Herbert as he would! He sat back, folded his arms and put on his legal look. Herbert maintained his speed stubbornly for a few seconds and then pulled to the side of the road. The motorcycle roared and stopped at the window.

"Who do you think you are?" the policeman bellowed at Herbert, who presented only his profile. "Can't you read? Don't you see what the signs say? Goin' seventy miles an hour!"

Herbert refused to reply. The policeman motioned to

William to lower the window. "Hey, you, whyn't you tell him to hold down his speed?"

"I have repeatedly done so," William said in a quiet voice.

"Whyn't you fire him?" the policeman demanded.

"He has been with us a number of years," William said.

The policeman snorted. "He'll lose his license a number of years if this goes on!"

William smiled. "I am afraid he deserves to do so."

The policeman was only slightly mollified. "Where you goin'?"

"I am due at the city hall at three o'clock," William said. "I am legal counsel in the case of The City of New York versus Marty Malone."

The policeman hesitated. "I oughtn't to let you get by with this."

"Perhaps I can get a ride with somebody and leave the car and my chauffeur with you," William suggested.

The policeman continued to hesitate. "No," he said finally. "I'll let you go this time." He leaned on the front window to attack Herbert again. "But you, fatface, if I ever catch you speedin' here again, and I'll catch you if you do, you'll lose your job sure. You won't have no license again for a good long time. Haven't I spoke to you before?"

"Maybe," Herbert said tightly. His small mouth disappeared between his cheeks.

"Maybe," the policeman mocked, "maybe for sure, I guess! Well, it's the last time. Now take it easy."

He waved them on, and William said nothing. It was possible that Herbert could be frightened.

Late at his office, he hurried to his desk and found a telephone call from Cousin Emma waiting for him. He was about to put it impatiently aside when he remembered her extreme age and fragility and his responsibility and so he ordered it put through. Across the city wires the trembling old voice reached his ears shrilly.

"William, is that you?"

"Yes, Cousin Emma, what can I do for you?" He glanced at his watch. At least she would not be long-winded. She was able to keep only one thing on her mind these days.

"William, I have had a letter from Jessica."

"What does she want?" he asked impatiently. Jessica was less than important at the moment.

"She wants to go home, William. She says she can't stand the horrid place. She wants to see her little baby. She says the baby ought to come home. She doesn't think they are treating the baby right. The baby doesn't even know who she is."

"I should think not," William said drily. "She has never taken care of it."

"Well, she wants to know," Cousin Emma said shrilly. "I think you ought to get her out of that horrid place."

"I believe Elinor has called up the doctor," he replied.

"What did you say, William?"

"Have you got your good ear to the receiver?" he demanded.

"It's no better than the other one now," Cousin Emma said.

"I say," he repeated in a clear low voice, "Elinor has talked with the doctor."

"That's good, is she coming home?"

"If she wants to," William said.

"Well, she wants to," Cousin Emma said.

"Then I suppose she is coming home," William said.

"That's good, I'll write and tell her."

"Better wait," William commanded.

"Didn't you say she could come home if she wants

to?" Cousin Emma demanded. "Well, if she wants to do so I suppose she can, can't she?"

"Yes," William said in desperation, "yes, yes, all right, Cousin Emma. You write to her."

He was irritated with the nonsense, and he hung up the receiver forcibly and plunged into the papers on his desk.

Nevertheless his irritation was touched with enough alarm so that he remembered the conversation when he reached home two days later and repeated it to Elinor.

"Jessica is coming home," Elinor said. "Didn't Herbert tell you?"

"Herbert isn't speaking to me, I think," William said. "He was stopped by a state policeman on the way down and I didn't exactly defend him."

"Oh, well," Elinor said comfortably. "I hope when Jessica gets home and the child is brought back that they can resume some sort of normal living."

They were not prepared, however, for the arrival of Jessica, Herbert and the child on the next Sunday morning while Bertha was at church. Bertha had become recently religious and was fetched every Sunday morning by a neighbor with whom she went to a church whose denomination she had never been able to remember, but where she found comfort enough to enable her to live through the week without having to recount with tears how wicked Jessica was to her old mother and how nobody at the orphanage really cared for the baby. She and Herbert did not speak, but otherwise their relations went on as usual. She made pitiful attempts to engage his sympathy, but his stubborn determination prevailed in his steadfastly ignoring her.

William, walking about the lawn with Elinor after breakfast, saw Herbert's new second-hand yellow convertible car come dashing up the road, and swerve into

the driveway. He turned his head away, expecting to hear
it crash against the heavy stone pillars of the entrance.
This it escaped, however, and Herbert brought it to an
abrupt stop in a swirl of gravel. Jessica, it seemed, did
not mind speed. She got out of the car holding by the
hand a small exquisite child in a ruffled pink organdy
dress and Herbert descended, smiling and proud. Jessica
herself looked actually beautiful, William saw with profound reluctance. He had a horrible chill of fear. What
if she should renew her false pretensions of a relationship
here and now? She came forward gracefully with her
usual modest air.

"Good morning, Mr. Asher, and Mrs. Asher, too. I am
so happy to see you again. It's so lovely to be home at
last. I told Herbert this morning that we must come
over the very first thing and thank you for everything. I
know they wouldn't have let me come home unless you
had both insisted."

The pretty voice was sweeter than ever, deepened
with an edge of sadness. Jessica's face, too, was more
delicate, more thoughtful, and her large blue eyes were
remote and gentle.

"Good morning," William said stiffly. But Elinor saw
only the child.

"What a beautiful little girl!" she said, and kneeling
down upon the grass, she took the child's small plump
hand. "What is your name, dear?"

"Monica," the child replied.

"Monica?" Elinor repeated.

"I have always liked that name, Mrs. Asher," Jessica
said, "though I never knew anybody called it. It came
out of a book. It was an English story, I remember."

"Come and sit on the terrace," Elinor said kindly. "I
shall find a cookie for Monica."

Thus in a moment they were sitting in the terrace

164

chairs, Herbert smiling and yearning, the sunshine glistening on his fat white face. Elinor disappeared and came back with a plate of cookies.

"Take a cookie," Jessica said almost sternly to Monica.

The child put out her hand and took one carefully by the edge, and stood holding it between her thumb and forefinger.

William remained silent, wishing that he could escape. He had no small talk for such an occasion. It was impossible to forget the repulsive scenes of the past, and yet it was incredible that they had left no mark upon Jessica except the slight pensiveness which only increased her grace.

"I hope you are home to stay," Elinor said cordially.

"Oh, yes," Jessica said with eagerness. "The house seems so nice. Herbert has tried to keep it clean. I do want the downstairs papered, a satin stripe, I think, something like you have, Mrs. Asher, in the parlors. And I think I shall have the sofas covered in velvet, a pale green, perhaps—what do you think?"

"It sounds very nice," Elinor said with reserve.

"Of course, if I had not been ill, we would have had the new house built by now," Jessica went on, hurrying a trifle more than she had used to do when she talked, with a slight blurring of the sharp consonants, and certainly her eyes were not steady. They darted here and there, restlessly, and suddenly she rose.

"Do you mind if I look over the dear old house, Mrs. Asher?"

"Not at all," Elinor said.

The child started to follow her but she said sharply, "No, no, Monica, you mustn't come—"

"She may if she likes," Elinor said.

"No," Jessica cried almost passionately.

"Here, baby, stay with Daddy," Herbert said. The child,

an obedient little thing, orphanage-trained, went and sat on his lap, but she did not taste the cookie she still held patiently in her right hand, careful not to soil her dress.

Herbert's eyes brimmed with tears. "I don't know how to say what I have to say, Mr. and Mrs. Asher," he began. The tears spilled and rolled down his cheeks.

"Is something still wrong?" Elinor asked to help him.

"It's my job," Herbert said. "I ought to stay at home. I oughtn't to be way off, maybe on the road goin' to New York, and leavin' her alone at night. I believe that's what set her off before, bein' alone at night, it was always late before I got home, and maybe not gettin' home at all some nights. A chauffeur's life is not his own, so to speak."

"Such a pity she won't have Bertha with her," Elinor observed.

Herbert wiped his face all over with a clean handkerchief and his voice hardened. "I see exactly how she feels about the old woman. Jessica is refined and Bertha is as common as they make 'em. An old German peasant, is what Jessica calls her."

"Do you know what a peasant is, Herbert?" William asked.

Herbert hesitated.

"Never mind," William said. "Only they aren't hateful, as a rule."

"Whatever Jessica feels for the old woman it can't be mended now," Herbert said obstinately. "She can't forget."

"Do you know, Herbert," Elinor said suddenly, "I don't believe that Bertha ever hurt Jessica one bit. Bertha has been with us for forty years and she has never hurt anybody. I have known her all my life and we used to tease her terribly when we were children and she never even got cross. She just used to laugh. She laughed a great deal in those days. Poor soul, she scarcely laughs at all now."

"She hurt Jessica," Herbert said stubbornly.

They did not argue. Elinor spoke to the child persuading her to taste her cookie and William sat silently smoking. Jessica came back after a few minutes, her eyes bemused. "It's all the same," she said softly, "just as I remembered it."

She looked strangely at Herbert. "I wish you'd go in the kitchen a bit. I want to talk privately to Mr. and Mrs. Asher."

Herbert got up, bewildered, letting the child slide to her feet. "What you got to say that's private?"

"Go on—go on!" she cried in quick passion, and stamped her foot.

He went away then humbly, pathetically so, William thought. Well, Herbert had tried beating her and now he was going to try love. It was quite obvious but, he feared, equally hopeless. Was Jessica really well? He watched her intense pretty face. She had seated herself and now she drew her chair close to Elinor.

"Dear Mrs. Asher, you both understand, but perhaps you will understand best. Is there any way that I can get out?"

"Get out?" Elinor repeated.

"Away, away," Jessica said with soft impatience. "It's terrible to live in such a deserted place as the farm. What is the use, Mrs. Asher? The work is all to be done over again every day. I cannot get to a theater, nor even to a movie. If we lived in a town at least I could walk up and down the streets and look in the shop windows. But there is nothing to look at where we live."

"Why don't you ask Herbert to take you into a town?" William asked. This was all ridiculous, the idea of having to spend a Sunday morning upon Jessica!

167

"He says an apartment of the sort I want costs too much. He says I would be dissatisfied, we couldn't have all our furniture."

"It is your mother's house, I believe?" William said. "That means you pay no rent."

She gave him a strange, cold look, as though she had not understood what he said.

"Jessica," Elinor said kindly, "if you could do exactly what you like best, what would you do?"

The pretty face, so delicately sad, flushed a pale rose. Jessica clasped her hands. "Oh, I would learn painting— it is what I have always wanted, to be an artist."

Elinor considered. She turned to William. "I don't believe that I ever told you Jessica does rather nice water colors. She used to paint her own Christmas cards."

"It has done me no good," Jessica said sadly.

He could see that Elinor was moved but he could not at all believe in Jessica. "If you really want to learn about painting," he said gruffly, "some of the finest artists in the country come to Manchester for the summer. I can easily get you lessons and perhaps for nothing. Why not?"

Her blue eyes flickered away from his face. "It's so hopeless, living where we do."

William was suddenly angry. "Look here, Jessica, stop talking like that. You live in a countryside where plenty of rich people pay money to live. Don't blame the place."

He feared for a moment that he had said too much. Jessica's face lit with anger, she trembled, but only for an instant, and then it was over. She restrained whatever impulse she felt, and her head drooped. "Thank you, Mr. Asher. I believe we ought to be going. I'll just call Herbert."

She disappeared between the open French windows, her slender figure so light that she made not the least noise, and they waited. The lovely child stood looking at them thoughtfully, not afraid, and yet not friendly, a child who had lived among strangers all its life.

The minutes passed. "What can they be doing?" Elinor inquired. But she did not go in to see, and after perhaps five or six minutes Herbert and Jessica came out again.

"Goodbye, Mr. Asher and Mrs. Asher," Jessica said formally. "It has been pleasant to see you. Do come and see us when you can."

"Thank you," Elinor said, bewildered.

"Come, Monica," Jessica said.

Herbert hesitated, and looked as if he must speak. He glanced at Jessica, walking toward the car. Then he leaned toward William. "She says, don't think you can make her take lessons. I don't know what she means but that's what she says."

William was suddenly outraged. "My God, it was her idea, not mine!"

Herbert looked unbelieving. "She says, sir, don't think you can make her do it, that's all."

He stalked away and climbed into the car and they whirled off.

"Did you ever hear of such impudence?" William demanded, glancing at the cloud of dust.

Elinor shook her head. "Let's forget them. They are both incomprehensible. I am glad that Herbert is leaving. Let's not ever see either of them again. The poor little child!"

She stretched herself upon a long chair and turning her face to the sun she closed her eyes. William, gazing upon her gradually relaxing face, felt the impulse to do the same. She had summed up his own conclusions about the human race, wherever one found its peculiar members. They were incomprehensible, in these times, at least.

Only history made them seem plain, the classes separate and orderly. Now blessed be the sun shining down upon him and upon Elinor as they accepted what they could not understand.

⚔

BERTHA walked stolidly up the gravel walk and they heard her footsteps and opened their eyes. She was hot and red, and under her toque of crumpled violets which was her Sunday hat they saw at once that something had happened. She paused at the step.

"Jessica and Herbert komm they here?" she demanded.

"They did, Bertha," Elinor said pleasantly. "They brought the little girl."

"I thout it wass so," Bertha muttered. "I did—I did, andt she dondt shpeak to me! She just sees me go by."

She went on around the house and they lay down again and closed their eyes to the sun, determined to forget.

"Amazing," William said, without opening his eyes. "Why do we have to have them? We pay them to do the work and they torture us."

"We are too easily tortured," Elinor said, without opening her eyes. "We ought to be ruthless."

They could not be ruthless, and that was the trouble. They remained human, and upon their tender human feelings, which could not believe that any creature born was purposely cruel or unjust, these ignorant ones trod, not knowing how they wounded nor caring. In a microcosm here was the world within the walls of his own house. They wished to live their pleasant lives, kindly to the suffering but not entangled. It was no longer possible. William felt an outraged anger sweep through his soul and run like heat through his body. He got up with an energy sudden and intense, and Elinor opened her eyes.

"What now?"

"I am going to fire Bertha," he said in deliberate calm.

"Oh, no," Elinor cried, "we mustn't—after forty years, William!"

"It should have been done long ago," he declared. "They've clung to the family like leeches, sucking the spirit out of us, feeding on our sympathy, justifying themselves by their impudence. I'll cook the meals."

"Don't be silly," Elinor said.

"I'd rather be silly than go on with this sort of thing."

She watched him in an awe of horror. She was a Winsten, that he could understand, and she had grown up under Bertha. Bertha had her big red hands on every part of the house, it was only Bertha who knew how many linen sheets there were, how many silver spoons, which were the heirlooms and which the wedding presents. Bertha who was supposed to be only the cook was actually the manager, the tyrant, the usurper, and in addition she fed upon their minds and souls, she took their precious time to listen to her woes, she clouded their happiness and destroyed their peace, and they had not had the courage to send her away, because they had been trained in kindness to those weaker than themselves. Well, he was going to put an end to it. It was absurd of course to say that he would do the cooking but there must be other cooks, and he would send them away one after the other instantly if they came out of the kitchen.

He stalked into that room and found Bertha tying a large white apron about her thick waist. Her full purple lips were quivering and the tears were running down her cheeks. She wiped them away with the edge of her apron.

"You vant somedings, Mr. Asher?"

"Yes, Bertha. I want you to go home." He said this in a mild voice that she took as kindness, his wish that she take a day off.

"I haf no home," she wailed, her face wrinkled like an old baby's and the tears welled again.

"Then find a home for old women and go to it," William said in the same steadfast and dreadful voice.

Bertha stopped crying suddenly, her jaw hanging. "You dondt mean you fire me, Mr. Asher!"

"I do," he said. "I mean it exactly."

Her tears dried in the instant. She snatched at the strings of her apron.

"I go, I go now!" she shouted in a high shrill scream.

"No," William said. "I'll drive you to Manchester."

"No, indeed no, you think I drive mit you? No, I von't. I call a taxi, I dondt rite in your *verdammt* car!" She was suddenly beside herself with rage. She clenched her fists and shook them in his face. He had expected a change but this was monstrous. Nevertheless he remained calm, watching her with curiosity. This was what she really was. Perhaps she *had* beaten Jessica. He could believe it now.

"You," she screamed, "you should neffer think you are a family here! You are nottings—a—a—" She spat upon the floor she had scrubbed so many thousands of times. "You a shentlemans! Ha—ha! I tell efferybody how you are. Efferybody will know you different."

"Nobody will believe you," William said inexorably. "Get your things together, Bertha."

"After forty years, you turn me out so," she moaned, collapsing on the wooden chair. "Heinrich allways told me, he says ofer and ofer, 'Dey turn you oudt, Bertha

172

ten, tventy, tirty, forty years, any day, dey turn you oudt, oudt.'" She snapped her fingers.

"Either you must get out or we must get out," William said gravely. "Since it is our house I suppose we will stay. You will get proper pay."

"Pay," Bertha screamed. "Who pays me back for years I scrub und vash und cook? Going to bed tired effery night?"

"We have paid," William said. "You have been paid in money and in time. You have had a home here and three meals and more a day. You have made your living easily among kind people."

She listened without comprehension. "I go," she said, sobbing. "I go now."

She climbed the stairs to her room above and he heard her moving about. His heart was beating with remorse and sympathy and good impulse and pain. But keep her here he would not. The house must be swept clean of them all. There must be no more Jessica, no more Herbert, no more Bertha, no more even of the piteous Monica. He could bear no more. He must get up in the morning knowing that he would see no stupid face, hear no sullen voice. They would buy machines, many more machines, and when the machines had done the work they would put the machines into the closet and close the door and live in the clean and quiet house where there were no human beings except themselves. The evil and parasitic life of servants would be cleared away, and they would be free forever of voices in the house. He telephoned for a taxi and then sat down on the high kitchen stool, while Bertha pounded to and fro above his head sobbing loudly and crying out to God in heaven, and he waited. Old family servants! They were no part of civilization here. The poison or the health of democracy, put it as one liked, had crept into them all, and

173

they rebelled against themselves while they served others more intelligent than themselves. They could not recognize the truth, that they were doomed by their own stupidity and by that alone, never to rise above the level of their birth. He felt that he was on the verge of discovering things important, though perhaps it was nothing more than the right of those like himself also to be free. The incubus of the stupid and the weak could become a tyranny as intolerable as any others, and should it not, like every other tyranny, be overthrown?

Before he could clarify this discovery Bertha came stumping downstairs with two suitcases and a huge bundle tied in a sheet.

He rose. "Your taxi will soon be here," he said with the same inexorable kindness. "I shall go and write a check that will do you for a couple of months. Within that time I shall compute carefully exactly what you should have as a pension. That money will be sent you every month on the first and the fifteenth, as soon as you send me your address. It will support you amply and in comfort at any old-aged home of middle range."

She made no reply, she sniffed back her tears and again he had to struggle with his impulse to relent. No, he would not relent. To do so would be to make freedom impossible. He walked from the room with dignity and went to the library and there wrote a check for five hundred dollars and blotted it carefully. Then he went back to the kitchen and put it on the table. "The taxi will soon be here. If you wish, please do come and speak to Mrs. Asher. She feels very sorry about this, but we have taken as much as we can."

"You take?" Bertha repeated in a sudden bellow. "It is me—me—" she beat her breast and burst again into angry sobs.

174

"I am sorry," he said gently. "I don't expect you ever to understand."

He withdrew then silently and went back to the terrace. Elinor was not there. He went indoors and called but there was no answer. He went upstairs to her room and tried to open the door. It was locked.

"Elinor!" he called.

She opened the door at once and looked at him with a queer abasement. "I suddenly felt afraid of Bertha. Isn't that absurd? But when you left me I realized instantly that I've always been afraid of her."

"She has never ill-treated you," he remonstrated.

"No, never, she wouldn't have dared. But though I defended her to Jessica, still I remember I used to feel when I was quite small that she would like to have smacked me, often. I wonder if she didn't smack the older ones? I never heard it said. My mother was very strict with the servants, and then of course when I was married, Bertha was afraid of you."

"Was she, indeed?" he murmured. He stood by the window watching for the taxi.

"Oh, yes," Elinor said, listening. She had locked the door again. "She told me once that you were 'the knowing sort.'"

"Meaning?"

"That you saw more than you told, I suppose. She's afraid of lawyers, anyway."

"Here is the taxi," he said.

She came to his side and they stood there. Bertha was waiting. She came around the side of the house lugging the suitcases, and sent the man for the bundle. They saw her climb into the cab, and then it whirled around the drive and out the gate.

"She did not once look back," Elinor said, half sadly. "The forty years mean nothing to her, I believe. Or perhaps they mean too much. Oh, William, how had you the courage?" They sank on the chaise longue side by side.

"I don't know. It does take courage to violate one's impulse toward kindness. But I was just angry enough. If one can catch the moment, always lasting only a few seconds in people like us, when indignant anger outweighs the habit of careful goodness, one has courage enough for anything. If I had waited five minutes until kindness undid me, I could not have simply ordered her off as I knew I must."

"Poor Bertha," Elinor said.

He refused to allow her to be sad. "Not poor Bertha at all. She has had a good job and a comfortable home for decades, and she will get a pension for the rest of her life. Lucky Bertha!"

Elinor shook her head, not disagreeing, however, he could tell by the softness and even admiration in her eyes as she gazed at him.

"My darling," he said, much moved, for how long had it been since she had so gazed at him? "This is a great day. Put on your hat and we will go out to dinner. A celebration, my love, is in order."

He was charmed with her swift obedience. She waved him away, signifying that a hat was far from enough, that she must change and look her best, and he went into his own room and examined his appearance in the mirror and decided upon a change for himself. He took down from its hanger his best grey suit and clothed himself in it, and chose a blue foulard tie. He saw with modest pride that he was growing handsomer with the years, his grey hair becoming his dark skin and there was no trace of baldness. His father had had a thatch of snow white hair, but he had worn a beard and Elinor did not like beards, a clipped moustache, very close, but no more.

Had his upper lip been a trifle shorter, Elinor had once declared, she would have demanded that he shave it.

He presented himself at her door and admired the trimness of her blue suit. "A handsome couple, eh?" he suggested.

She smiled a ravishing youthful smile, indicative, he felt, of her inner rejoicing. Ah, they were going to be happier! He should have rid the house years ago. Might he not have changed the whole course of life had he done so? The cloud would not have come between Edwin and Vera; Winsten, his elder son, would not have looked at him with the hidden doubt so often now in his eyes, kept alive, William felt sure, by the unforgetting silence of Madge. And Susan, ah, Susan might never have married Peter! He was convinced after long pondering in the magnifying small hours of many nights, that Susan had not made up her mind quickly, that it had taken the brutal terrifying moment when the black dog sprang at Pete, to shock her into deciding for him, a perverse atavistic admiration to which modern girls were increasingly prone as the traditional shelter fell. It did not bear thinking of, not now, at any rate. He would take it out again and again in the night when the darkness hid him and ponder upon the monstrous damage that had been done to his family. Then, too, he must reflect upon whether the damage could be mended, and how, their lives changed, they could be restored.

"Where shall we dine?" Elinor was asking.

"Let us set forth and find a place we never saw before," he said. "Let's be made all new, in honor of fair freedom."

Arm in arm they fell into step and marched smartly down the stairs.

Six weeks later on a rainy morning in court he was approached by a clerk who broke in upon his presentation of the witness Arturo Romano, a bookie.

"Excuse me, sir," the clerk whispered. "There is an urgent call for you."

William waved him away with his black-ribboned pince-nez. "I cannot be interrupted."

"Excuse me but somebody's dead—a member of your family, sir," the clerk said.

A member of his family? William appealed to the judge for a brief recess, simply repeating what the man had said, for what else was there to say, and striding through the astonished and staring crowd, he reached a telephone in the adjoining room.

"Mr. Asher—that you?"

He could not recognize the hoarse voice, nor even if it were a woman's voice or a man's.

"Yes, it is," he replied.

"It's me—Bertha."

"Where are you?" he demanded. "What happened?"

"Mr. Asher, sir, Miss Emma—*tot!*"

"I am coming at once."

Cousin Emma! He flung himself from the room, staying only to tell the clerk to report that he would come back when he could. He caught a cab and ordered the man uptown to the apartment.

Cousin Emma had had a bad heart. She was very old, close actually to ninety she must have been. Still nothing excused him for not having been near her for weeks. Elinor had visited her last, actually, and Edwin had talked of going but propably had not. Perhaps Vera was the one who had gone most often to visit her, since she and Edwin had moved into the city to live, so that he need not commute to the office. Edwin was still in the office, delaying his years at the law school, uncertain, it seemed, as to what he wanted to do.

But why was Bertha the one to call him, William asked himself, unless indeed Cousin Emma, with her unfailing kindness, had taken Bertha in? He paid off the taxi and went into the house. Nobody knew, apparently, the doorman was calm, the elevator man was indifferent. He dreaded the entrance, but forced himself sternly to the door. It opened and Bertha stood there, a solid figure in a dingy black suit, her hat awry and her straight grey hair hanging in wisps about her face, a pasty white.

"I komm here," she panted. "I chust come here and she is *tot*—"

He pushed past her down the wide hall to the bedroom. The doors to the living room and dining room stood open, and in a window a canary sang its soaring, trilling song.

"Where is she?" he asked.

"Im bedt," Bertha whispered. "She didn't get up yet. She chust lies—"

He opened the one closed door and saw Cousin Emma. The room was frightfully close, the shades drawn and the heavy long curtains pulled over them. There was some sort of sweet perfume spilled. Everything was in disorder, silly disorder, not like Cousin Emma who was always neat. She lay high on two big pillows in a shape

179

of agony, her knees drawn up, her withered arms bare and distorted, the lace sleeves flung back. Then the light fell on her open eyes. He saw two bright metallic dots glitter suddenly in the very center of her dark pupils. He gave an involuntary groan, and turning on the bed light he stooped and examined her motionless eyes. The two glistening points were indeed metal, the ends of what looked like headless nails, or no—knitting needles! Cousin Emma was always knitting. Someone had thrust deep into each eye a fine thin knitting needle, and blood and fluid had run down her cheeks in two glutinous streams, scarcely dry.

He was sick with horror, his tongue curled in his dry mouth, he could scarcely restrain himself from pulling out the needles, thrust so deep that he saw instantly they must have penetrated the brain.

"Was she like this when you came in?"

"Yes, chust the same," Bertha whispered. She put her black cotton gloves to her lips.

"When did you come?" he demanded.

"Chust before I called you, Mr. Asher. I run right avay qvick to telephone. The girl in the office sayss you are in court and she vants to know vot iss, but I dondt tell it. I sayss I muss myself tell to you. But some mann in court sayss he muss know, before he vill call. So to him I chust sayss some vomans in family is *tot*."

No use to feel the heart in that stricken ancient frame, the limbs caught in their astonished writhing. There was no life here now, so little had there been before. He turned to the telephone and called Cousin Emma's doctor, nevertheless, and then hesitating he called Edwin at the office.

"Edwin?"

"Yes, Father."

180

"Come at once to Cousin Emma's apartment. She has died suddenly."

Edwin was too well trained to ask a single question. "I'll be there at once."

William closed the door and called Bertha into the living room.

"Bertha, listen carefully and answer me. How is it that you are here? I thought you were in Mount Kisco, in that home."

"So vass I," Bertha said.

"Sit down," William commanded. The canary, impelled by their voices, set up his quivering silver-edged music. "Why did you come here, Bertha?" William asked.

Bertha shook her head. Her thick red hands trembled as they clutched her black gloves.

"You must answer me," William said. "Otherwise you will be accused of murder."

The purple lips trembled. "Mr. Asher, sir, *bitte*, help me—"

"I can only help if you tell me the absolute truth," William said sternly.

"Jessica, sir," Bertha whispered, her sobbing breath drew inward. "She vass here."

"Jessica?"

"Ya, she vass—"

"How did you know?"

"She telephoned me she candt shtand Herbert again and so she tells to Miss Emma and Miss Emma says komm here, and so she is here and she says Miss Emma tells me to komm today and she vill to talk mit me. And I thout Miss Emma vants to talk Jessica and me to friendts again, and I vass happy and I komm so qvick."

"Was Jessica here when you came?"

"Ya," Bertha moaned. "She vass."

"And how did this happen?" He glanced toward the closed bedroom door.

"Ya—it chust happens," Bertha moaned. "We fight, Mr. Asher. Jessica fights me. She opens the door und I am in, und she stares, so—"

Bertha widened her eyes frightfully and glared across the room at nothing.

"And then?"

"Und dann she shcreams at me how she hates me, und she vill kill me. I dondt lissen, she didt alvays talk so to me if nobody is mit uns, but I tellt her, 'Be qviet, you make soch a noise for Miss Emma.' So Miss Emma hears us und she kooms oudt the bedt, and opens the door and tellts to Jessica, 'Dondt talk so badt to poor old Bertha.'"

Lies or truth? Lies or truth?

"Und Jessica shpeaks sudden so nize," Bertha went on, sighing in gusts, "she sayss, 'Miss Emma dear, get back in bedt, your foots are cold,' and so she goes in mit, und I vait and I vait so long. Und Jessica comes oudt and I am making a liddle coffee and she says, 'I go now to drugstore to get some pills Miss Emma iss needing. You vait, please.' So nize she talks! So I vait and I vait, und she dondt komm back, und Miss Emma is so qviet, and so I open the door und I see!"

It was then that he called the nearest police station.

Lies or truth? William examining the fat purplish face could not tell. Forty years had made a mask of flesh. The doorbell rang and Bertha got to her feet by habit at the sound and opened it. Edwin was there.

William rose. "Come in, my son. Come into the other room." He hesitated. Should they leave Bertha, would she try to escape as Jessica had done? But Bertha had sat down again, a heavy almost sodden figure overflowing the straight wooden chair.

"We'll be back in a few minutes, Bertha," he said.

"Dot's all right, Mr. Asher, I vait," she said heartily. She folded her hands, still clutching the black cotton gloves.

William led the way in to the closed bedroom, shielding Edwin, dreading for him the sudden sight of the contorted figure on the bed. Death was dreadful for young eyes and yet all must see it sooner or later. He went directly to the bedside and lit the table light again.

"Do you see her eyes?" This question he put in his normal voice.

Edwin bent to look, his face went white. "Father, how horrible!"

"Jessica was here. But what purpose could there be? That's what we must find out."

"Does she need a purpose if she's mad?"

William did not reply to this. "On the other hand," he went on, "we have only Bertha's word for it that Jessica was here."

"I can't believe Bertha would have the courage for this," Edwin replied. He moved away from the bed, out of sight of the twisted old face.

"We don't know what Bertha is," William said. "I have never told you how violent she was when I sent her away. And Jessica, you know, has always maintained that her mother was cruel."

"Jessica lies and you know it," Edwin cried out.

Ah, William thought, then the wound still remained!

"You don't believe what Jessica says, do you, Father?" Edwin demanded.

"Of course not," William said. He crushed down deep in his mind the knowledge that anything might be true, anything at all. He had seen strange sights in his life as a lawyer and he had heard stranger lies than those Jessica had told even against himself. But Edwin, intuitive beyond either of his other children, felt the reservation.

"You will not grant that absolutely Jessica is a liar," he said bitterly, and then came his revelation of the cloud. "Neither will Vera. She says she is sure that Jessica lied, but she will not say she truly believes that she did. I have to live with that."

"It is very wrong of Vera," William said. "If I hesitate it is merely my lawyer's training which commits me to permanent doubt, even about myself." He decided suddenly to comfort Edwin in the best way that he could, the most self-sacrificing and the most profound. He felt the blood mount to his face, slow and red. "As a matter of fact, Winsten told me that Jessica had made some equally absurd allegations about me."

Instantly he saw that Winsten, or Madge had told Edwin. His face, still so young, could not hide the knowledge, his eyelids fluttered slightly, the look in his eyes grew shy, the very shape of his face changed subtly to signify that he knew.

William tried to speak lightly. "I suppose you boys talked it all over and laughed at the fix the old man was in."

"We did talk about it, sir," Edwin said manfully. "Madge told Vera and me one night when we spent the week end there. I told her that if she ever mentioned the—the matter again I would never speak to her as long as I lived. I told her I was sure it was all lies."

"But you do believe it possible?" William asked quizzically.

The door bell rang loudly again and again before Edwin could answer and they went out together, William closing the door behind him. Suddenly he felt exhausted, almost faint. Bertha was opening the door and down the hall they could see the doctor and with him the police. "Look here," William said urgently to Edwin, "I am going to turn this whole dreadful business over to you. I'll go home and break things to your mother and get in touch with Herbert to find Jessica."

"Very well, Father," Edwin said with assumed composure. There was no time now to answer the question of believing.

William took up his hat and stick and walked down the hall. He shook hands with the doctor and bent his head slightly to the two policemen behind him.

"Now that you are here I shall leave my son in charge," he said gravely. "The deceased is my wife's second cousin, the servant is an old cook in our family, recently retired. She will explain for herself how she happened to be here. If I am wanted my son can reach me. I should go home to be with my wife. My son is in my own law firm and is well qualified to assist you."

He nodded to receive their assent, hurried out of the house and telephoned at the drugstore next door for his car.

The journey home was welcome to him; he needed time to consider what must be done. The new chauffeur, a Vermont farmer's son enamored of the city, drove silently and with a certain *élan* of pleasure in his job. He was still unmarried, and it was enough to have freed himself from the farm. His young enthusiasm filled him with zeal and the desire to please. This, too, would wear away as all else did but it was enjoyable to William while it lasted and today a blessing.

In the vacuum of time moving through space William's legal mind worked quickly and well. He outlined to himself a clear line of action, step by step, which he intended to write down for Edwin's benefit. Bertha, or Jessica, must be defended but the case could not remain with their firm. His mind played over the roster of the city's lawyers and he chose one headed by an old college mate and friend, Barnes, Holt, Mackintosh and Lane.

185

When the long hours drew to their end and he saw the roof-lines of his home back in the early dark and caught the flow of lighted windows through the trees he felt strong again. He was always strong when he knew what he ought to do.

Elinor met him at the door when he reached home. It was late but she looked so fresh and pleasant that he dreaded to destroy her mood. But it must be done. They kissed, and he put his arm about her.

"My dear, you must prepare to hear a very distressful thing."

Her mind flew at once to the children, the tender grandchildren, the younger ones, as though death always threatened them most nearly. "Is it the children—"

"No, not the children. The oldest person in the family instead—Cousin Emma. My dear, she died very suddenly this morning."

"Oh no, oh William—all alone?"

"Come into the library, Elinor."

There, when she had sat down, very simply he told her what he had found and exactly how he had learned about it.

She was appalled, unable to grasp the full evil of what had happened. It was not death that disturbed her, he could see, for Cousin Emma was so old, but it was the manner of death and the monstrous contrast to Cousin Emma's unfailing goodness.

"She was so good," these were the words she kept repeating. "I cannot imagine why—when she was so good, especially to Jessica, always to Jessica. She always said that we must be kind to Jessica because she was the child of the cook and the butler. She said we must not let Jessica feel any difference. I shall never understand it, Cousin Emma, of all people—do you remember how she thought Jessica should not marry Herbert?"

"We must not be sure that it was Jessica," he warned her. He rose and went to the telephone and called Herbert. The country exchange was slow and he listened lest one of the maids interpose with some household call, but at last he heard Herbert's heavy voice.

"Well?"

"Herbert, this is Mr. Asher."

"Oh, hello, Mr. Asher."

"I am calling from home, Herbert, to inquire how Jessica is."

He waited during a long second or two. Then Herbert said, "Jessica's pretty good, Mr. Asher."

"She's still at home?"

"Yeah, she's here." Herbert turned his head and his voice grew distant but was still clear. "Want to talk to Mr. Asher?" Quite clearly, too, he heard Jessica's peevish reply. "What should I want to talk to that old fox for?"

Herbert's voice was at the mouthpiece again. "She's here busy at something—looks like knitting, I guess."

"You haven't moved to a town after all?"

"No, we ain't goin' to move."

William hesitated. How put the question he needed to have answered? "Someone told me that Jessica was in New York and I wondered if it were true."

Herbert's slow voice repeated the words, "In New York? She ain't been in New York. How'd she get there? I didn't take her."

Herbert's head turned again. "He says you was in New York, Jessica, haw haw!"

"Dirty old beast," Jessica's voice said sharply. "Tell him to mind his own dirty business."

Herbert's voice came back again. "Jessica says tell you no she wasn't in New York. Guess she would like to be, though, but I ain't got the time now with all these chickens on my hands."

"Do I hear your little girl's voice?" William asked pleasantly. He had heard a wail and a slap.

"Yeah, she's just got into something, I guess."

"Well, I won't delay you," William said and hung up. This was very bewildering. Was Jessica lying, was Herbert shielding her? "Herbert says she was not in New York."

"It doesn't matter," Elinor said most sadly. "Poor old Cousin Emma, such a true gentlewoman, if that means anything anymore—I don't know! Only it wasn't fair for her to die like that—so terribly frightened at the end—I can't think of it." She put her hands to her face and hid her eyes.

"Don't think of it," William said. "Only remember how much happiness she got out of being good and kind. She could not have been anything else, whatever the end. She fulfilled her own nature."

"And now Jessica has fulfilled hers," Elinor exclaimed. Her hands dropped to her lap.

"Wait," William reminded her. "We must find out the truth."

The day of the funeral was such a day as Cousin Emma herself might have chosen. Her aged body, distorted by autopsy, was restored again to decency, washed and clothed, her white hair curled skilfully to cover all scars. Her eyelids were drawn like shades over the tragedy they concealed, and she was housed in a handsome casket of mahogany with silver handles. The family plot was in the Manchester cemetery and the place was crowded with strangers. Few of Cousin Emma's friends had survived to come to her funeral but the dreadful story of her death, flashing through the newspapers, brought scores of cars speeding from all directions.

The family, standing about the open grave, took no notice of the curious crowd except that Elinor, glancing about, said in a low and wretched voice, "How she would have hated this!"

For Cousin Emma did not truly like the common crowd. Scrupulous and delicate in her approach to every human being, she shrank from the many, and lived, it must be said, as a recluse for most of her life, thereby magnifying the value and the meaning of the few persons she knew. But this was her public end, the newspapers screaming the details, and Bertha and Jessica both under arrest.

It could not be prevented. Herbert had come begging to William. "You're a big lawyer, Mr. Asher, you get crooks a trial when everybody knows they're guilty. Here's Jessica locked up when I can swear she was at home. I've had to put the baby in the orphanage again. Bertha ought to be locked up, she was right there, but Jessica wasn't. I can swear—"

"The matter is quite out of my hands," William had said firmly. "It is not possible for me to handle the case."

The minister was dropping the clods, crumbling them to earth, and letting them fall. "Dust unto dust—" his intoning voice went on, and a bird burst into sudden song in the elm tree above his head. What, William wondered senselessly, had become of Cousin Emma's canary? It had been forgotten. Winsten's little girl, the third child, began suddenly to cry. She should not have come, he did not approve of children at funerals but Madge had insisted that it was a family occasion, death as well as birth, and that the children ought to know.

They were all there except the baby, the fourth child, the boy.

The funeral was over at last, and local police parted the crowd for the family to walk through to their cars. The family went home alone and closed themselves into the house and the crowd went away again, discussing the guilt of the cook or the maid, betting upon one or the other, while the grave was covered with the displaced earth and then massed with flowers. Not many people remained to give Cousin Emma flowers, and William and Elinor had sent a blanket of white roses and maiden-hair fern which made a good show. Edwin's and Vera's pink lilies were at the foot, and Winsten's and Madge's yellow roses at the head. A few people from the crowd had thrown down wild flowers, a homegrown rose, stalks of delphiniums, a handful of daisies.

Cousin Emma was of no importance, William reflected, merely a woman who had lived a kindly, good and somewhat lonely life. But that she had died by violence, that she could be murdered, was significant indeed, and by such a death she became important.

ON A CERTAIN spring morning, years later when the pattern of life had been pleasant long enough so that William had all but forgotten Jessica, when the Christmas roses Elinor had planted on Cousin Emma's grave were already in bloom, he received a telephone call. It was Saturday morning and he was at home after a late breakfast.

"Who is it?" he demanded.

"It's me, Mr. Asher."

"I don't recognize you."

"It's Herbert Morris, Mr. Asher."

A violent revulsion dashed William's spirits. Why must he hear this voice again?

"Good morning, Herbert," he said with hypocritical calm.

"How are you, Mr. Asher?" Herbert asked.

"Very well, thank you," William replied and was not deceived. He expected the next question.

"Mr. Asher, I wonder could you do something for me?" Herbert was humble indeed.

"I don't know, I am sure," William replied.

"Could you and Mrs. Asher please go to see Jessica, sir, and tell me if you don't think she's well enough now to come home?"

William was stunned at the monstrous request. Was Jessica to rise again from her living grave? Was her voice to be heard again in his house? "I cannot see that it would do any good whatever, Herbert," he replied at his stiffest.

"You see, Mr. Asher, sir," Herbert said with all his old submissive stubbornness, "she looks real well, just like she used to. She talks sensible-like, too. She'd like to come home. She says we ought to be united again. The child is growing up without a mother, sir."

"It is not so simple for Jessica just to come home, Herbert," William said in his gravest voice. "You forget what has happened."

"I'll never believe it was Jessica—who did for Miss Emma, sir," Herbert said earnestly. "If it wasn't Bertha it was some stranger crep' into the house. Jessica couldn't do no such thing as that. She can lose her temper and bite like a kid or somepin' like that, but she couldn't murder nobody. Why, I always had to kill the chickens for Sunday dinner. She'd run in the house and shut the door and put her hands to her ears, she'd cover her eyes so she couldn't look out the window and see it floppin'."

"That doesn't change the jury's verdict," William said.

"Well, sir, Mr. Asher, you're a lawyer. You could maybe get the governor to give a pardon—give her another chanct, like. We could maybe even get another trial."

William wavered. His legal mind was touched. He had known prisoners unjustly accused and imprisoned for years. Bertha's exoneration and Jessica's sentence were sound enough, but there were loopholes that no one had been able to explain. Though he had remained determinedly a spectator, except when called upon as a witness, he remembered clearly the weak points of the trial.

"And Jessica hates that asylum somethin' terrible," Herbert pleaded. "She says it turns her stummick to see all those old crazy people, when she ain't crazy herself. And another thing, Mr. Asher, they work her like anything. Soon as they found out she knew waitress work they put her in the dining room where all the doctors eat and she has to wait on 'em and she don't get no pay for it. 'Course they don't want to let her go. It's natural they don't. But is it fair?"

The newspapers in recent months had carried stories about mental institutions, heartrending enough to stir now in William's memory. It was possible that in the huge institution where Jessica was sheltered there were such iniquities, though why, he groaned to himself, need they be his concern, or she, for that matter, a concern he had always unwillingly assumed.

"I will talk to Mrs. Asher," he said, evasively.

"Thank you, Mr. Asher," Herbert said with the quick cheerfulness of the uncomprehending mind. "I sure will appreciate it. You're kind of a big man around here, I guess you know, and they might listen to you while they don't pay no attention to me at all."

The morning was spoiled, William thought gloomily. He had no intention of helping Jessica to get free and yet his wretched sensitive conscience had been stirred again and he knew of old that he would have no rest until he satisfied it. He hung up the receiver and returned to the library where he had been working, but not to his desk. Instead he sat down in the deep window seat facing south where the sun poured in, and saw Elinor in the garden below. He wished he need not tell her of Herbert's call. She looked calmly happy down there in the peony bed, in her old green serge suit. Oh, what a plague could grow within a man's contented home! He recalled, with utmost distaste, the way Bertha had looked at the trial, on just such a sunny morning as this, too, only the sunlight strained through the huge dirty window of the city court room.

She had been called to Miss Emma's apartment, Bertha had declared, by Jessica, her daughter. The matron of the home, summoned as a witness, had confirmed this. Bertha had come downstairs in the morning of the murder dressed to go to town. She said she was going to see a relative of her former employer. She had then taken the bus in front of the home. The matron, a pale exhausted middle-aged woman of a faded genteel appearance, had given the further information that the bus did not use to stop so handy but she had got them to do it, so that her old people would not have to walk in the rain or stand waiting in the cold. "They can come out of the house when they see the bus comin' and get in like it was their own private conveyance," she said, a mild pride brightening her languor.

On the other hand, Jessica had been so entirely herself that William still found it difficult at this moment to face certain questions secret in his own mind. When Jessica had been called upon to rise that day at her trial, she had done so with an air almost sprightly, and with the graceful light step he knew so well she had gone to the stand. Obviously, as he still remembered, she made an appealing impression, her grey suit and lace ruffled blouse, the small grey felt hat on her blonde hair had all the air of a lady, and one still young. As long as she lived, he supposed, Jessica would look young. She had held spotless white kid gloves in her right hand and there was a small pink rose on her lapel. Lifting her head, she had looked about the room, smiling faintly, and the pallor which was habitual to her passed into a sudden delicate flush.

"Is there any reason," the attorney asked very gently, "why you should have disliked Miss Winsten?"

Jessica drew in her breath. "Oh no, sir! On the contrary, she was the kindest member of the family—to me, at least."

"You had known her many years?"

"All my life."

"When is the last time you saw her?"

"I went to see her, sir, after I got out of—one day after I had come. I had been ill and had been sent away. Miss Emma helped to bring me home again when I was quite well, and then I went to see her."

"How did you get there?"

"I walked to the bus, sir. It's only about a mile from the house. It goes straight to Manchester and there I can always get a train."

Herbert had started up from his chair and had put up his hand like a boy in school but no one heeded him. He sank back, the sweat pouring down his cheeks.

"Do you usually take the bus?" the lawyer asked.

"Oh yes," Jessica said brightly. "I always do, Herbert never takes me anywhere. He's so busy."

"Your Honor," Herbert had shouted at this, getting to his feet.

"Sit down!" the judge thundered. Jessica's head drooped.

"Did you take the train on the morning when your mother says you were at Miss Winsten's apartment?" the lawyer asked Jessica.

She had lifted her head proudly. "I am sure I did not."

"Yet you know, that if what you say is proved true, your mother will be charged with murder?"

"I am saying what's true," Jessica said with frank composure. Then she added with a sad smile, "My mother and I have not spoken in years."

William had stirred and coughed. Now was coming the story of the childhood beatings, the cruelties, all the wicked accusations which might or might not be true—

"My mother," Jessica said touchingly, "was very cruel to me as a child. She locked me in the cellar and when I cried she beat me. I could show—there are still marks on my body of these blows. When I was only seven years old she sent me to a convent in Canada, and I did not see my father except once a year, in the summer. I loved my father and he loved me. Then he died. My mother was cruel to him, too. Miss Emma could never believe it, no matter what I told her."

Sitting in the library window seat now, years later, William suddenly understood that last declaration. He remembered how Jessica's face had changed, had hardened as she spoke these words. She had been opening and shutting the latch of her small handbag nervously and suddenly she snapped it shut with a perceptible click so that he could hear it even where he had been seated far to the side. Of course, of course that was why she

had killed poor Cousin Emma! The gentle old lady had
sent for her to plead with her once again, for Bertha's
sake, to be reconciled. Cousin Emma had never forgiven
him for discharging Bertha. He remembered very well
when Elinor told him about that. She had gone to see
Cousin Emma on one of her usual visits, and had told
her where Bertha was and why, and Cousin Emma had
been quite distracted about it. She had exclaimed over
and over again, "But Elinor, my dear, one has an obliga-
tion to an old servant!"

"Bertha is very comfortable, Cousin Emma," Elinor had
assured her.

"Oh, but it is the heart that needs comfort," Cousin
Emma replied. "I shall send for Jessica, I shall certainly
talk to her."

This she had done more than once, William knew,
and although he himself told her it would be of no use.
But Cousin Emma was incorrigibly softhearted, the more
so as she grew older, and so he had not tried to persuade
her. He supposed she must have seen Jessica several
times, perhaps many times. And doubtless on that final
morning she must have persuaded her too much, she
might even have accused Jessica of lying, and at that
Jessica's mind burst from the cage in which she tried
to keep it imprisoned and hidden.

That day at the trial when she declared her mother
cruel, people had stared at Bertha, but she sat immobile, gazing across the room at the tall windows. The
jury had leaned forward to listen to Jessica, always sympa-
thetic, and the questioning went on, until she was finished. Then she sat down and put her white lace handkerchief to her lips.

Bertha had not moved. When her name was called
she had started and stared about her as though it was
for someone else.

"Come, come," the lawyer said, "get into your place."

She had got to her feet, a thick bewildered figure. She had moved to the stand and taken her oath in a voice so low that it could not be heard. Then clutching the wooden rail, she had waited, gazing humbly at the judge.

"You have heard the accusation of your daughter?" the attorney said.

Bertha gave a massive sigh. "Ya, Jessica talks so—"

"Is it true?"

"I neffer beadt my little childt," Bertha said somberly. "Sometimes I slap her a liddle bit venn she runs in the big haus, ya. There she dondt belong. So muss I teach her, her papa wondt. To beadt—no, neffer!"

She stopped, as though no more could be said.

The questions went on relentlessly. "How did you come to be at Miss Winsten's apartment?"

"Jessica calls me. She tellt to me Miss Emma vants I shouldt come. Miss Emma tellt to me before that some-time when Jessica is home we muss be friends und I say 'Ya, gewiss, vy nott?' So I vish, but Jessica von't. Iss maybe because she is sick in the headt she dondt vish, I dondt know."

"Sick in the head?"

"Ya, they sayss so. I dondt know. They take her away and put the baby in a orphanage. Herbert, he vill tell to you. I dondt know."

Herbert had been recalled and questioned. Unwillingly he had given the ugly story of his life with Jessica, her reluctance to grant him his rights, the final struggle, and trying to conceal all he told everything.

William could not bear the memory. He got up and went out into the garden to Elinor. She was on her knees by the peony bed the better to see the pushing young shoots of the peonies.

"They have come through the winter, after all," she said happily when she saw him. She had felt much concern for the peonies, always delicate in the severe Vermont winters, and coaxed through only by the aid of shelter and manure. He came and stood by her side, contemplating the thick rose-red shoots.

Then he told her, grumbling after every sentence, "I do not see why, when things are peaceful, Bertha comfortably senile in Mount Kisco and Jessica locked up safely, we should again stir up everything."

She smiled ruefully, "Except that you know we will, and the more we hate to do it, the more we'll feel we ought. We can't put down the burden. We'll have to go and see for ourselves how Jessica is. Think of the child! Poor Monica—"

They were silent for a few minutes, Elinor on her knees, carefully, with tender fingers, removing the crusts of winter earth from around the shoots, while William watched. He was remembering again, not really watching, recalling unwillingly the last time he had seen Jessica. She had been pronounced insane, and Bertha had been exonerated upon her steadfast and unshakable story. He stooped to touch Elinor's shoulder. "Then you think we had better see Jessica?"

She sat back on her heels and looked up at him and he was startled to see, in the heartless light of the morning sun, that fine wrinkles were now clearly about her eyes and lips.

"Once more," she said gently. "Then perhaps your conscience will rest."

He nodded. Ah, she understood him!

The upshot of it was that the next morning, it being Sunday, they decided to make the visit to Jessica instead of going to church, "a good deed instead of a profession," William put it wryly.

The new chauffeur, as they still called him, was accustomed to them, and drove them at a safe and quiet rate the thirty miles to the huge mass of buildings where Dr. Bergstein expected them. William had telephoned the evening before, and the cordial doctor had agreed to be present when they arrived. He was in his office, a bare small room whose walls were lined with file cases and text books, a short kindly looking man, William remembered, whose kindness was nevertheless always cool and businesslike.

"Come in, Mr. Asher, good morning, Mrs. Asher. Please sit down."

They sat down, he took his place behind the desk, and put on a pair of gold spectacles. "I have just been refreshing myself in the case of Jessica Morris." He riffled some papers on the desk. "There is really nothing to report. She was much disturbed when she was placed here three years ago by court order, as you know. She did not respond well to shock treatment, but we gave her hydropathy with good results. At first she refused to work but for the last two years she has worked efficiently and well in the staff dining room and has even taken over the ordering of food supplies. She spends her leisure, I note, in the occupational therapy room and does rather nice water colors and some textile designing for the patients. The occupational therapist reports her intelligent and cooperative."

William's spirits sank. "Does this mean that she is well?"

The doctor shrugged his thick shoulders and spread his hands. "Well? What is well? Here she functions as a well person would. More we do not know."

William exchanged looks with Elinor.

"May we see Jessica for ourselves?" Elinor asked.

"Certainly," the doctor said. "In fact, it is almost time

for luncheon. Why not come to my table and lunch with us? Then you will see Jessica at work."

"An admirable idea," William said.

A few minutes later they followed Dr. Bergstein down bare endless corridors to a rectangular dining room set with many small tables. It was a cheerful room, as it had need to be, William thought. There were flowers on the tables, tastefully arranged.

"The flowers are also Jessica's work," Dr. Bergstein said. "She has a nice taste, very sensitive. Also, obviously, her background has been among cultivated people. She reads books, her English is beautiful. Sit down, please. Let us see if she recognizes you."

He rubbed his hands with sudden enjoyment, his professional curiosity aroused by the new situation.

"There she is," Elinor exclaimed.

Jessica stood against the wall among the other waitresses, easily the most striking among them. Their uniforms were clear blue cotton with white aprons and small white caps. The color was becoming to Jessica, her fair hair was loosely curled, cut short now instead of piled in braids upon her head in the old German fashion. She had lost her extreme thinness, her figure was nicely rounded and yet slender. Her face was alive, her lips red, her bright blue eyes alert.

"I never saw her look so well," William said.

"She is well because she is happy," Dr. Bergstein said. "Yes, here she is happy. She is busy, she tells some others what they should do, she arranges the flowers, she enjoys the library. People like her very much. Sometimes a man likes her too much and then she comes quickly to tell me so, and I must speak to him." He laughed. "Jessica is very moral, very virtuous. She is always reminding everybody that she is a married woman."

"Does she want her husband to visit her regularly?" Elinor asked quietly.

Dr. Bergstein pursed his fleshy lips. "No, I cannot say so. At first she would not see him at all. Then because he has a car and takes her for a drive, with special permission, she began to allow this. Sometimes she will not see him for months. But still," he laughed again, "she is a married woman. It is a protection. She will always want protection while she has her own way. Ah, that is very normal."

Jessica was looking at him and he waved. Suddenly she recognized them. Her face brightened with smiles, she came with her old graceful swiftness across the floor, her step as light as ever.

"Oh, Mrs. Asher, dear!" she cried sweetly. She seized Elinor's hand and held it in both her own. "You have come to see me at last, and Mr. Asher, too. Oh, I told Herbert only last week how I wished I could see your faces again! You haven't forgotten me?"

"No, indeed," William said. "How are you, Jessica?"

"Oh, wonderfully well, thank you, Mr. Asher, only longing to get back to my own little house and see my darling child, such a tall girl now, and she needs her mother, I know. How is Mr. Edwin—and Mr. Winsten and Miss Susan?"

"All well, thank you, Jessica," Elinor replied.

They were dazed, she had forgotten everything, or had she really? She was the same warm, young-looking creature, her pretty face pink and white and unlined, her eyes clear.

"You had better bring some food, Jessica," Dr. Bergstein said in good humor. "We are hungry."

"Oh, yes," she exclaimed in her soft eager way. "How shameful of me! I am forgetting my duty." She took their order carefully and tripped away.

"Well," William said, "well, well, well!"

Dr. Bergstein shrugged again. "You see? Who can say?"

"It is very confusing," Elinor said, troubled. "If she is herself again she should not be here."

William could not speak. The prospect of Jessica's future was insupportable, if indeed she was well.

She was back again very soon, and with exquisite service she set before them the dishes they had chosen.

"I remember how you like lamb chops, Mr. Asher," she said playfully. "I had these turned once more for you, knowing you enjoy them well done."

"Thank you," he said.

It was a good meal, simple but well cooked, and William ate it although he was not hungry, replying now and again to some remark of Dr. Bergstein's. Elinor carried the conversation while he caught fragments of it.

"Jessica looks quite different from the others," she was saying.

Dr. Bergstein agreed. "She is different—a very complex case. Very interesting!"

The meal was over at last. "Would you like a little while with Jessica alone?" the doctor asked.

William was about to refuse but Elinor spoke first. "I think I would."

"Then please come into a sitting room for guests. We have one upstairs that is quite private. I will send for Jessica to meet you there."

He led the way and William muttered to Elinor behind his back, "Why on earth must we see her alone? I've had enough."

"Hush," Elinor said.

In a sitting room with vivid green upholstery and curtains they sat down and waited in silence. There was much to say to each other, each felt it, but this was not the time. It was not the end of the visit, no conclusions could be made. The room smelled of dust and a peculiar acrid reek that William could not diagnose. He rose and opened a large window, not easily. It had not been opened for a long time.

In ten minutes or so there was a tap on the door. "Come in," Elinor called.

It was Jessica, her uniform changed for a suit of thin navy blue wool with white ruffles at the breast and neck. She looked, as William saw very unwillingly, extremely pretty and she stood hesitating before them, her unchanging smile still on her face.

"Sit down, Jessica," Elinor said.

She sat down then on the straight-backed wooden chair and crossed her narrow feet, encased in black patent leather shoes. William, who seldom noticed women's clothes, noticed these also. It was astonishing that Jessica could have so maintained herself here.

"Well," William said, "Herbert wanted us to come and see you and so we have. We'll tell him you are looking very well."

Jessica dimpled nicely. "Oh, Herbert," she cried, laughing. "He should be ashamed, troubling you! I told him so. But he knew I was longing to see someone from the family." She turned suddenly wistful. "I suppose Mr. Edwin is very happy?"

"He is," Elinor said firmly. "It is a very successful marriage."

The slight cloud was swept from Jessica's face as though by an invisible hand. "And the dear little children, Mr. Winsten's little children, are they well? So big now, I suppose, and I wish I could see them."

"There are five of them now," Elinor said. "I believe Madge wants six."

Jessica shuddered. "Oh no, Mrs. Asher, how can she? It's so dreadful."

William stared at her. "What do you mean by that?"

Jessica laughed again and put up her hand to smooth her hair. "Oh, I don't know, Mr. Asher, I suppose I shouldn't say it. I'm always saying things. Is the house just the same, Mrs. Asher?"

"Quite the same," Elinor said. "We have two very nice young women to help us."

"I wish it were I who was helping you, Mrs. Asher," Jessica said, wistful again. "I should so love it."

"You don't like it here?" William asked.

Jessica shivered and then suddenly covered her face with her hands. "No!" she cried in a small sobbing voice. "I hate it—I'm just a prisoner! They work me—so hard—day and night. I don't get a penny. It's just being—a slave."

William gave a great sigh. He sat back in his chair and looked at Elinor helplessly. Elinor raised her eyebrows. What can be done now, the eyebrows asked.

Jessica was sobbing softly. "I miss my baby so! I've hardly been with her at all—just a few weeks. A child needs her mother. I feel her needing me. But I'm helpless."

William could not endure more. "Look here, Jessica," he said with sudden authority. "If this is the way you truly feel, if you think you can behave yourself and not torture the life out of everyone, for what reason I cannot imagine, because all of us have been kind to you always—"

"Oh, yes, Mr. Asher," Jessica breathed. She lifted her face, rosy with weeping. "You don't need to say that—I never forget anything!"

"Well, then," William went on, "if you want to try again to be a decent reasonable woman, I will see what I can do to get parole for you, at least that. If we can prove that you are well, if you can behave yourself at home, it may be that you might some day be pardoned."

"Pardoned for what, Mr. Asher?" Jessica asked like a child.

"You told me just now that you forget nothing," William said harshly.

"If you mean Miss Emma, sir, I didn't do that," Jessica said in the same eager soft voice. "I was at home with Herbert that very day, all day, or very nearly. It was the day before that I went to see Miss Emma, but that was the day that he was so awful. He tried to—he was like a beast—he—oh, I can't say it! I cannot put it into words! It's—it's indecent. Before the baby, too! I always slept in the baby's room, and he came in anyway, though he had promised—"

He waited, holding his breath, but her fearful sensitive mind felt something dangerous in the silence. She straightened her back with an effort and said in her usual voice, "Such things I try to forget, but kindness I cannot forget. Miss Emma was the kindest person of all—to me, that is, and I loved her. I could not have hurt her. But she never would believe what I said about my mother. It was true, it was true, but Miss Emma wouldn't believe me. Why, even on that last day—"

"What last day?" William demanded.

Jessica's flush faded instantly. "The last day I ever saw her, the day before she died—"

He decided on the final test. "Very well, I am glad to know you want to go home to your husband and child. You seem quite well. I see no reason why you should not go home on parole. I will give my own guarantee that you are well enough and I can, I think, persuade the doctor to release you on parole after the proper permission has been given." He was making a promise impossible to perform, the law could not so easily be set aside, but it was a test which his instinct told him could be risked. He met her eyes fully, concentrated upon his, and allowed her a moment to comprehend what he had said. Then he asked the question, "Would you like to go home at once, today, with us? Herbert would be pleasantly surprised."

"William!" Elinor said. Her voice was a low warning. "You are going too fast," the voice implied, "you are imposing a shock. Besides, suppose she accepts, how would you perform?"

"Now?" Jessica echoed in a high tight voice. She sprang up, her whole body stiffened, even her hair sprang electrically from her head, her eyes dilated, glittered, stared. She screamed, "Oh, you can't make me!" And swinging out her arms as though she were about to fly she ran to the window.

"William!" Elinor cried.

He leaped from his chair and caught Jessica by the waist. The door opened and Dr. Bergstein came in, strode across the small room and seized Jessica's flailing arms. "Excuse me, I have waited outside. I was afraid of something. So, Jessica, you want to jump out of the window this time." He pulled down the window with a bang. "We never open the windows, Mr. Asher. Now, Jessica, be calm." A nurse in a white uniform came instantly at the touch of his hand on the button set in the wall. Jessica began to cry loudly at the sight of her.

"Jessica," the doctor said, "it is no use. Again, after two years, but it is still no use. Take her to the hydropathic room, Miss Baker."

"Yes, Doctor," the nurse replied.

They heard the dreadful wild sobbing receding down the hall, the frightful screams.

"Is she being hurt?" Elinor said anxiously.

"No, Mrs. Asher," the doctor said. "Do not worry. She

206

is not being hurt. She feels she must scream. We see the other Jessica."

They sat down shaken and for a moment were silent. Then William said with a solemn sadness, "Doctor, I have one more question to ask you."

"So many questions I cannot answer," the doctor said. "I will try this one more." He waited, while the sunny afternoon was wasted.

"Could anything have been done to prevent this?" William asked. "Was some mistake made when she was a child?"

"He means," Elinor interpreted, "could we in the big house have acted somehow differently to Jessica when she was small? Jessica was the daughter of our family cook."

Dr. Bergstein spread his hands and he gave again the heavy shrug. "Who knows? It is a question. But Jessica was born the child of the cook, was she not? She did not wish to remain the cook's child and so she hates the cook, who is nevertheless her mother. She wishes to be a child of the big house, like you, Mrs. Asher, but she is not, and so she hates you. She does not dare to hurt you, because here is Mr. Asher to take care of you, so she hurts a poor old helpless lady, who is also belonging to the big house. She thinks she is in love with a young man in the big house, so that he can bring her into the world she wants to belong to, but unfortunately the young man does not love her. But Jessica does not really love anybody, you know. That is her tragedy. And so all your kindness and goodness—I see you are very kind good people, Mr. and Mrs. Asher—does her no use, for it makes her only to wish that she too was so kind and good, and she knows she is not but she does not know why, and she thinks it is because she is not really one of you, body and soul. She wants to be born again, Mr. and Mrs. Asher, but it is sad

207

we can only be born once. She knows she is a stranger in your house."

They listened to the stout Jewish doctor, speaking from the depths of his own unknown life and hidden experience, and his words fell upon them with the dreadful impact of truth.

"We can never be rid of the burden of Jessica," William said at last, very somberly.

"No," the doctor agreed, "it is true. Being what you are, good people, you cannot be rid of the burdens. You take them and you keep them—but, my dear sir," he leaned forward and put his hand on William's knee, "this is the hope of humanity! If good people can forget, then indeed there is no God."

They rose and the doctor looked at his watch. "Oh, heaven, it is four o'clock nearly. I promised my wife and children—yes, please excuse me. And you are quite satisfied now that Jessica must stay here?"

William hesitated and cleared his throat. "But one more question—do you think Jessica is really insane, Dr. Bergstein? In the technical sense?"

The doctor gave his shrug and spread his hands once more. "Technical? What is that? It is a meaningless word to me. Jessica is not always insane, no, not when she is enjoying her life." He smiled and glanced about. "Here is a big house, too, is it not? A very big house, a very big family. She is more pretty than most of this family, more clever, she is like a sort of princess here, therefore when she is thinking such things she is not insane, not at all. But take her away, put her where she does not wish to be, a big house where she cannot enter except as the child of the cook, and yes, I will say she is insane." He paused and stood, very kindly and solid, fastening upon them the shrewd, assessing, humorous warmth of his gaze. "We may say, my friends, that Jessica is suffering from the effects of democracy. So, if I may say it, are you."

He bowed, smiled, and went away with surprising nimbleness for so large a man.

William stood still for the matter of half a minute, digesting the doctor's last words. He perceived their profundity and did not wish to talk about it. "Come, my dear," he said, turning to Elinor. "Come home. There is nothing more that we can do for Jessica."

They went home in silence almost complete, and when they got out again at their own door, they mounted the steps side by side, somewhat wearily. The house was quiet enough as they stepped into the door. But someone's coat was flung upon the chair by the long oaken table, someone's soft tweed coat and a small round red felt hat with a black pompon of feather caught at one side.

"Susan!" Elinor exclaimed, crossing the hall. "What does this mean? Susan!" she called up the stairs.

Upstairs a door opened, and Susan stood there at the bannisters above them and looked down upon them. Her dark short hair fell on her cheeks, and her large dark eyes made her face pale.

"Where did you come from?" William demanded.

"I've come home," she said.

"Without Peter?"

"Without Peter," Susan said.

Their hearts sank together, his and Elinor's. He could feel the downward plunge in her bosom as clearly as in his own.

"We'll come up," Elinor called, her head tilted back to gaze anxiously at the pale face looking down at them.

"I'll come down," Susan said.

They hung up their wraps soberly, accepting in mutual silence whatever was to be. Then they turned to their daughter, and standing side by side, they regarded her.

### Voices in the House

They were not prepared for the sudden torrent of Susan's love and pity. She stood before them, quite self-possessed apparently, looking at them, one face and the other, and then suddenly she spread her arms and embraced them both.

"Oh, please don't look like that," she begged. "You make me feel ashamed. You're bracing yourselves, I can see it. You needn't, darlings, nothing awful has happened. It's just that I—well, I had to have time to think and I found I couldn't think unless I came home quite by myself. Where have you been?"

She squeezed herself between them, clinging to an arm of each, and in three they walked toward the east parlor and as three they sat down on the long sofa.

"We went to see Jessica," Elinor said.

"Why on earth—" Susan began.

"Herbert thought she might be well," William broke in. "I am glad we went to see for ourselves. She will never be well, the doctor made it quite clear. She can only be well if she stays where she is, protected, successful, you might say, in her own way. She cannot cope with life as she has found it. She has neither the strength nor the wit for it, but she does not know that."

"What an extraordinary thing!" Susan exclaimed. Her eyes, very thoughtful, did not leave his face. She was thinking, thinking—

"I begin to see the strangest light—a curious twisted sort of light," she said slowly, "but coming somehow from Jessica, here in our house, and shining in the queerest way upon Peter—and me."

She leaned forward between them and buried her face in her hands, but she was not weeping. In an instant she threw back her head and got up, lit a cigarette from the side table and flung herself in a chair by the fireplace opposite them.

"Did you ever see Jessica here in this room, before the mirror?" she demanded.

"Never," Elinor said in surprise.

"I have," William replied.

"Oh, she was often here," Susan declared, "and all alone. We used to watch her when we were kids, Edwin and I. I don't know if Winsten ever saw her. But Edwin and I used to creep down the stairs and watch her when she didn't know. Sometimes we giggled and ran away, and then she cried. We were beasts—all children are. Once when she was here on vacation I went in my room and found her wearing my best party gown. Remember that pink tulle? I gave it to her after that, but she was frightened and wouldn't take it anyway. She said she'd never have a chance to wear it, except like that, here in the house."

"Poor thing," Elinor said, "but all the same it was outrageous."

She was severe, for she was more than tired of Jessica. She could not forget what Dr. Bergstein had said—"If good people can forget—"

"I do declare," she went on suddenly turning to William with a sort of passion, "I wish that we hadn't this big house, or any money, or even any education. I wish, actually, that we were savages of some sort. It's the ignorant and the uncivilized who really own the world today, I do believe, simply by being a burden to the rest of us."

"Oh no, they don't." It was Susan, speaking in the quietest voice. "Not at all, Mother! You are quite wrong." She began to laugh a soft subdued bitter laughter. "Remember," she asked, "remember how I married Peter for shelter, my dears? Remember how I thought him strong because he killed the black dog?" She added mockingly, "With his bare hands, my dears?"

211

A woman, this Susan, his daughter, William saw suddenly with a thrust of pain at his heart. The child was gone, and gone, too, was the young girl. She was a woman facing her life and seeing it as something entirely different from what she had thought it was.

"And what do you think," she was demanding of them now. "What do you think my Peter is? Not a rock, if you please, not a shelter, but a confused rough child, a boy who is so big he has to shave his beard by day but at night he is afraid of the dark. I don't mean really the dark, not anything as simple as that, but afraid of knowing what he is, ignorant and crude and empty inside." She was smiling, not with mirth but with a fearful sense of the desperate comedy of human life. "Yes, I've found that out now, too. But he comes to me for shelter, if you please. He wants to leave the garage. He hates the house he grew up in, he wants to come here, my darlings, where you could never abide to have him. He thinks we have it easy. That's what he says. He imagines that we know secrets that he doesn't—silly, isn't it? He thinks that if he knew all we do he would be powerful—as he thinks we are—and secure, as he is sure we are and as he isn't. He insists that he has as much right as we have to know enough to win, as he puts it."

To this outpouring William listened, astonished and cautious. What was it, indeed, but that most hateful word, *revolution?* A light illumined his comprehending mind. He saw Peter not alone but one of a vast and piteous company, pushing upward by any means they could into the wider spaces of a world they imagined was above them. So Jessica had tried to do, blindly and stupidly, seeing that world only in the shape of his own house, God help him, from which they had all shut her out, and had to shut her. Still, they might have understood her dreams, so childish and absurd, since for her dreams she lived and now was all but dead. Beyond her tragic shape he saw the shadowy faces of criminals he had defended and had heard condemned, all struggling and contriving and contending for that upper air.

Dreams! They were the living breath of every human soul and when they died, the soul died with them. What if his own dreams had never come to life? What if there had not been this house and all the love it had contained, or what if his dreams had exceeded the power of his brain to make them true? What if he, as Peter put it, had never had his chance, his right to know enough to win?

The past remained and Jessica herself was buried there. Yet let the past do its work, at least for Peter's sake. How could he explain to these two women whom he loved, who waited for him to tell them what to do? He chose to speak to Susan.

"You should be proud, my dear. You have done something wonderful for Peter, by loving him and marrying him. He is awakened. Of course he belongs to the family. We are all with you—and him."

He turned to Elinor. "We must get behind this boy, my dear. All that business with Jessica—it mustn't happen again, not in this house!"

He was not sure from the look on her face whether she understood, perhaps, not altogether, not yet—

But Susan, who never wept, began suddenly to sob. "I know what you mean!" She rolled her handkerchief into a ball and stabbed at her eyes. "I didn't think you could. Oh, Dad, thank you!"

He was distressed by her tears and then embarrassed, and he hid himself behind his usual dignity. "Don't cry, Susan. The fact is, I don't doubt I shall enjoy knowing Peter better."

His daughter wiped her eyes at this, she gazed at him

213

with a tenderness he had never seen before, and then inexplicably she laughed, softly, richly.

"I wonder if you realize," she said irrelevantly, "how absolutely precious you are!"

There could be no such thing as a happy ending to a lot of trouble. That, of course, he was too old and seasoned to expect. But the way was clear and he cleared it himself finally by a midnight talk with Elinor. She came into his bed that night as though she were lonely, and suddenly she said, as though she had been thinking about it for hours, "I love you, William, but I don't really see how we can undertake Peter! He can't be changed now. It's too late. The differences are too deep."

He slipped his right arm about her with accustomed ease, and drew her head to his breast.

"I don't think we should try to change Peter," he said. "That would be a mistake, and, as you say, impossible. I propose simply that as a family we open the house to him."

"I can't imagine Madge—"

The name of Madge recalled his mind to a slowly forming purpose.

"Darling," he said above her head on his breast, "this is a good time to tell you that I have for the past few years been uncomfortable with Madge because she half believed some absurd things that Jessica said about me."

"About you?" Elinor lifted her head, and looked at him in the dimness of the night light.

"Jessica once told Madge and Winsten that I had made love to her." He found the greatest difficulty putting this nonsense into words, not because he any more feared Elinor, indeed, tonight he feared nothing at all, but because his taste, trained to fastidiousness by generations behind him, shrank in disgust. Therefore he spoke the words baldly and quickly, denying himself the familiar luxury of silence.

"How absurd," Elinor said, "and why didn't you tell me long ago? It explains—Madge has been so strange with me sometimes, almost as though she felt sorry for me." She sat up. "It makes me angry, rather!"

"At me?" he asked quietly.

"No, of course not! What do you think?"

"You've said some things to me, you know," he reminded her.

She crept down beside him again. "I know—I can't understand why. There was something wrong in the house."

"Voices," he acknowledged and he stretched his arm about her again. Yes, there had been strange voices, disturbing, corrupting, cutting across the human grain of their common life. Yet Jessica herself had only been some sort of instrument, possessed, people would once have said by a devil, and yet there was no devil in Jessica, no devil perhaps anywhere, except the reverse energy of dreams denied.

"Anyway, you know me now," he said reasonably to Elinor. "You can help to bring Madge back into the family, and Winsten will come back with her."

Elinor opened her eyes. "Winsten never believed you had—"

"Not quite," he agreed, "but somehow as Vera believed Jessica about Edwin, all the time thinking she didn't."

"Now, William, Vera didn't—"

"Not quite, but enough to make Edwin feel that perhaps she did."

He felt something wet upon his bare breast. Elinor's tears! He rubbed her cheek gently with his left palm.

"Now, now," he said, comforting.

215

"I hope I can keep from hating Jessica," Elinor murmured.

"You can't hate her," he replied. "It doesn't do any good. That's why I want to get the family here under one roof so we can all understand things together."

"Jessica has been a dreadful burden," Elinor insisted.

He considered, remembering the moment when suddenly in the east parlor today he had felt the illumination of his soul. Such light could not last, of course. But he could remember it and he could live in the understanding light of memory.

"Well, yes," he agreed. "Jessica has been a burden. But then we kept trying to bear it as a burden. This was the mistake. We didn't just—let her into the house."

"How could we?" Elinor demanded. "She was a servant—"

He winced and interrupted her. "Hush, don't say that word, my darling. She just happened to be born Bertha's child. Anyway, it's Peter we must think of, now. There's still time for Peter."

And he braced himself for whatever that might mean.